GABRIELLA LEPORE

THIS IS WHY WE LIE

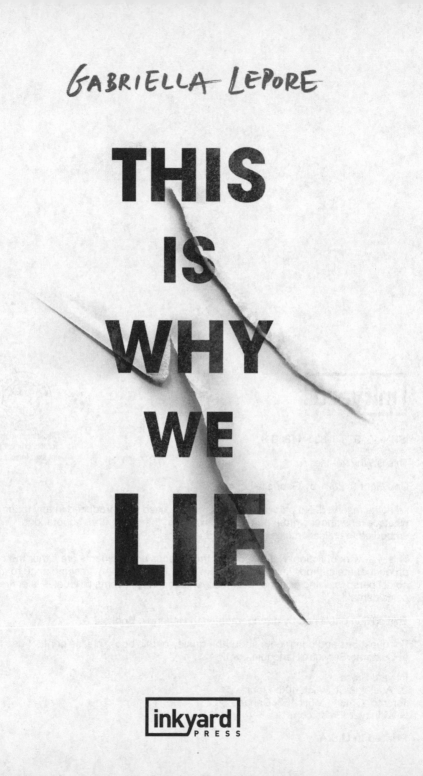

inkyard
PRESS

This edition published by arrangement with Harlequin Books S.A.

For questions and comments about the quality of this book, please contact us
at CustomerService@Harlequin.com.

Inkyard Press
22 Adelaide St. West, 40th Floor
Toronto, Ontario M5H 4E3, Canada
www.InkyardPress.com

Printed in U.S.A.

To Mum and Dad, with endless love and gratitude.

JENNA

Gardiners Bay at dawn is my secret. There's a moment, right before the day starts, when the ocean is bathed in amber light. That first golden breath of morning. Everything is still, apart from the pelicans gathering near the water, their plump bodies shuffling along the shoreline. Sometimes I sit on the promenade for hours with my legs suspended over the pebble beach below, just watching the night turn to day. Watching the darkness turn to light.

It's often like this, just me and the birds. The only other people I tend to cross paths with at this hour are fishermen wearing heavy-duty gear and hugging their thermoses. They sit on the benches and swig their hot drinks while skimming the daily newspaper. Then they leave. A little while later, their boats drift out onto the water.

Today, though, I'm the only one here.

I raise my camera and adjust the focus, capturing the new light as it spills over the ocean. In the muted daylight, the silver tide is a murky, dull gray and frothing as it slaps against the shore.

"Help! I need help!"

My eyes dart across the shoreline. There's a boy on the stretch of beach at the foot of Rookwood Cliff. He's knee-deep in the water, fully dressed.

He shouts again.

I spring to my feet and run along the promenade. Ducking beneath the boardwalk railings, I jump down to the pebbled cove.

The soles of my feet sting at the impact of the stones beneath my Converse. I scramble toward him, my footing slipping on the damp pebbles.

It's then that I recognize him.

Adam.

His jeans are soaked to the thigh. He's wading through the shallows, his legs tangled in fishing net and seaweed. And a body lies limp in his arms. A girl. She's swollen, her skin has turned purple, and one arm is swinging downward with the momentum of Adam's labored movements.

I press my hand to my mouth.

"Call an ambulance," he shouts.

But all I can do is stand there, paralyzed by the sight. He lowers the girl onto the sand and begins CPR, breathing into her mouth.

It's too late, I want to tell him.

She's already dead.

ADAM

Cops are swarming the beach, cordoning off access to the cove. Somehow, even in the chaos, there's silence. It's familiar, like some weird déjà vu shit, like I've been here before.

I stand beside her. Jenna, that's her name. She wraps her arms around herself as the wind whips at her long red-brown hair. She's shivering.

I am, too. My clothes are still wet, and my jeans feel heavy. They're rough and cold against my skin, weighing me down.

At the shoreline, two paramedics are moving Colleen's body onto a stretcher. One of them zips the body bag shut. They lift the stretcher and start making their way across the beach, heading toward the ambulance that's parked along the promenade.

Jenna releases a shattered breath.

I take her hand. It feels cold in mine. "You're okay," I tell her. But I'm lying.

A cop approaches us. I figure he's probably in his late forties, with graying hair and a heavy mustache. His eyes skate over me. The look makes me tense. I swear I can hear my pulse thumping fast in my ears, drowning out the hissing breath of the surf.

"Jenna," the cop says. Her fingers squeeze tighter around mine as she nods back at him. "Your aunt has been radioed. She'll meet you at the precinct."

"Okay." Jenna's voice is weak.

"You'll both need to come down to the station. Someone will take your statements there." His stare lingers on me for a second longer. A second too long. "You might want to call your folks. I'll give you a minute." The pebbles crunch and stir beneath his feet as he walks away.

Jenna's hand slips from mine. She waits a beat, watching me. The misty morning light catches the paler shades of green in her eyes.

"Aren't you going to call anyone?" she asks.

I shake my head. "Got no one to call."

One of the cops gives us a ride to the station. We sit silently in the back seat, listening to the occasional crackle of the police radio, with muffled voices spouting out codes and jargon. It's too humid in this car, and the seat covering squeaks whenever I move.

I've been here before. Different car. Different cop. But I've been here before.

Jenna reaches for my hand, and I flinch on impulse. It throws me for a second, but I catch her hand before she pulls it back.

I turn to her. She's tugging at her seat belt.

"You're okay," I tell her again under my breath. I force a smile. Or whatever expression I can muster to make her think that I'm calm. That this really is okay.

She gives me a small nod back.

The car slows as we reach a stoplight. The radio crackles again.

"Ten…confirming…body found…female."

Jenna draws in a shallow breath, and I run my thumb along the back of her hand, reassuring her.

It's okay, it's okay, it's okay. You're okay.

Maybe she doesn't want my comfort. She might not want me holding her hand and feeding her lines, like everything's fine. Maybe she doesn't want that.

But it's all I've got.

Interview with Jenna Dallas,
conducted by Detective Drew Felton at 10:20 a.m.
on Saturday, September 29th.

D.F.: How are you holding up, Jenna?

J.D.: I'm okay. I think I'm okay.

D.F.: Are you ready to start? If you need a minute...

J.D.: Yes. No. I'm okay.

D.F.: All right. We'll carry on. Just let me know if you need a pause.

J.D.: Thanks, Drew. Sorry—I mean, Detective Felton.

D.F.: Jenna, talk me through what happened this morning.

J.D.: I was on the boardwalk. It was early.

D.F.: Early?

J.D.: Six. Maybe six thirty.

D.F.: What were you doing out at six o'clock in the morning?

J.D.: I go to the waterfront to take photos sometimes. I'm trying for an art scholarship.

D.F.: Does your aunt know you do that? I can't imagine Kate is happy with you wandering the streets before dawn.

J.D.: (inaudible.)

D.F.: You're going to have to speak up, Jenna. Does Kate know you head out to the boardwalk that early?

J.D.: Yes, she knows. She's fine with it. We only live a couple of blocks away. Gardiners Bay is safe. I always thought it was safe, anyway.

D.F.: Take me back to this morning, Jenna. What happened when you were on the boardwalk?

J.D.: I heard someone shout for help from Rookwood Beach. I saw Adam, so I ran to him. He had Colleen. He was carrying her out of the water. I didn't recognize her at first.

D.F.: You know Colleen O'Dell from Preston Prep School?

J.D.: Yes. She's in my senior class. We weren't friends, but I knew her.

D.F.: You weren't friends?

J.D.: No, I mean, we weren't *close* friends. We weren't enemies or anything. I just didn't know her all that well.

D.F.: Let's rewind for a second. You said you saw Adam Cole go into the water to get Colleen?

J.D.: Yes. Well, no. I saw him come *out* of the water with her.

D.F.: But you didn't actually see him go in?

J.D.: No, but he was helping her. He went into the ocean to get her. To save her.

D.F.: You didn't see that, though?

J.D.: No. Does it matter?

D.F.: I just need the facts.

JENNA

I take a seat on one of the plastic chairs in the precinct's waiting room. My hands fold around the warm disposable cup I got from the coffee machine. I've been clinging to my dollar latte for a while, but I can't seem to bring myself to take a sip. I'm pretty sure I'll barf if I try. My stomach isn't ready for anything. Not yet.

Across the room, Adam is staring out the window, drumming the glass with his fingers. His brown hair is still mussed from the sea breeze, and his jeans are still damp from the knee down.

Adam is a Rook, one of the guys from Rookwood Boarding School. I've met him before, but I can't say I know him. The school and its students are kind of elusive. The campus is tucked away from the rest of Gardiners Bay, set on what used to be some grand estate surrounded by acres of forest. After the estate was foreclosed, it was turned into a reform school for kids with behavioral problems. That's the official term. I guess it's a nice way of saying Rookwood is the last stop before juvie.

He catches my gaze. "You think we'll be here much longer?" His wet sneaker taps on the linoleum floor.

I glance over at the abandoned reception desk. "I don't know. I hope not. What else do they need from us?"

He squeezes his eyes shut. "Everything," he mutters. When he speaks again, his words are clearer. "I'm sorry I got you involved in this. I shouldn't have called you down to the beach."

"Are you kidding? This isn't your fault. Honestly, I'm glad you don't have to go through this alone." The memory of Colleen's body flashes through my mind. "I'm glad neither of us has to." My stomach heaves again.

"Thanks," he murmurs.

One of the ceiling bulbs flickers and hums. Suddenly, this room feels stifling, suffocating. I need fresh air, any kind of air—anything that isn't polluted by the bitter smell drifting from the coffee machine.

Adam crosses the room and drops into the chair beside me. "Are you okay?"

"No." I choke out a laugh. "Are you?"

He doesn't answer. His broad shoulders hunch, and he burrows his thumbs into his sleeves. There's a scratch on the back of his hand creeping out from the hem around his wrist. There's something else, too—the edge of a tattoo, snaking down from his forearm. It looks like a talon. Fitting, I guess. For a Rook.

"You're shaking." His deep brown eyes are back on me now and clouded with concern. "Do you need me to go get someone?"

I take a breath and ball my hands. "I'm okay."

He lowers his gaze. "You should talk to someone about what happened today," he says. "It'll help."

I stare up at the flickering bulb. "Really? More talking? I don't even want to think about it anymore, let alone talk about it."

We fall silent, and the bulb continues to hum.

"It gets better," he says after a moment. "It takes a while, but it gets better."

I swallow against the dryness in my throat. "How do you know? Have you been through something like this before?"

"Something, yeah."

We both jump as the door swings open and my aunt, Kate, paces into the room. She's wearing her police uniform, and her wavy brunette bob is pulled into a ponytail.

"Jenna." She envelops me in a hug. "Are you alright?"

"Yes," I reassure her. "I'm fine." When she pulls back to study my face, I force my lips into a strained smile.

She tilts her head. "Drew said you were there when Colleen was found."

"I was on the boardwalk. I went to help." I glance at Adam. His eyes are fixed on his sneakers. He doesn't say a word.

Kate's gaze wanders over him before returning to me. "Sounds like you both did everything you could," she says, touching my arm. "I'm going to take you home now, okay?"

My shoulders sink in relief. I try to catch Adam's attention again, but his focus is still on the linoleum. "Do you need a ride, Adam?"

He looks up, and his dark eyes lock with mine.

"Actually," Kate says to him, "Detective Felton still needs to see you. It won't be too much longer."

He rubs the nape of his neck. "Yeah. No problem."

"I can stay," I jump in. "I don't mind waiting."

Kate frowns, and Adam shakes his head.

"I'm good," he says. "Don't worry. You should go home."

"Detective Felton will be right out," Kate assures him, and he nods.

As Kate ushers me toward the exit, my chest tightens. *I can't leave him*, I want to blurt out. *We're in this together.*

His focus stays on me as I walk away, and his jaw clenches. I think he feels it, too. That sinking realization that he's on his own now.

Interview with Adam Cole,
conducted by Detective Drew Felton at 11:15 a.m.
on Saturday, September 29th.

D.F.: Adam, I'm just going to ask you a couple of questions. That alright with you, son?

A.C.: Yes, sir.

D.F.: Adam, why don't you go ahead and talk me through what happened this morning?

A.C.: I was on Rookwood Beach, and I saw this girl... She was in the water, a little way out. She was floating, facedown, caught up in some fishing net. She...

D.F.: Are you able to continue?

A.C.: Yeah. Sorry. So I called out to her, "Hey, you alright?" but she wasn't moving.

D.F.: This is when she was still in the water?

A.C.: Yeah. I swam out and freed her from the net, and I brought her to shore.

D.F.: And what time was this?

A.C.: I don't know. Around six o'clock this morning.

D.F.: What were you doing on the beach at six o'clock in the morning?

A.C.: Sometimes I can't sleep.

D.F.: Okay. Tell me, Adam, did you recognize the girl once you'd brought her to shore?

A.C.: I'd seen her around.

D.F.: Can you give me her name?

A.C.: Colleen, I think.

D.F.: What happened after you pulled Colleen from the water?

A.C.: I called for help, and a girl came from the promenade.

D.F.: Her name?

A.C.: Jenna. I don't know her last name. You already spoke to her, though.

D.F.: And what happened once Jenna arrived on the scene?

A.C.: You already spoke to her.

D.F.: Humor me. I'd like to hear it from your perspective.

A.C.: Jenna called for an ambulance while I tried to resuscitate Colleen. She stayed with us. With me.

D.F.: Right. You can take a break now. I might need to speak with you again at a later date. How does that sound?

A.C.: Yeah. Fine.

D.F.: Can I get your address, son?

D.F.: Adam? You heard what I said?

A.C.: Yes, sir. It's Rookwood. I live on campus.

D.F.: Oh. You're a student at Rookwood Boarding School?

A.C.: Yeah.

D.F.: I'll need to pull your records from the system. That alright with you?

A.C.: Yeah. I figured you would.

JENNA

"The body of missing schoolgirl Colleen O'Dell was discovered in the early hours of Saturday morning on Rookwood Beach. Police are treating the death as suspicious and investigating anyone who may be connected to the victim—"

"Shit."

Kate's voice makes me jump.

I hit pause on the remote, and the TV screen freezes. The reporter's expressionless face stops midsentence, her coral-toned lips parted as she stares deeply into the camera, transcending her world into ours.

Kate stands behind me, her eyes glued to the screen. I'm not used to seeing her on weekday mornings—she's normally at the precinct before my alarm even goes off. I quickly check the date on my phone to confirm what I already know: it's Friday, which means she should be at work. But judging by last night's makeup smudged beneath her eyes, she overslept. It was bound to happen eventually. She's been pulling all-nighters practically every day since Colleen's body was discovered a week ago.

"Shit," she says again.

"Are you alright?"

She turns away and paces across the living area. She pauses at the kitchen counter and frantically sifts through a stack of papers, undoubtedly searching for her work phone.

"Goddamn reporters," she mutters, raking a hand through her wavy hair. "Those details were leaked."

She abandons the countertop and starts digging through her purse. Morning sunlight is streaming through the tall windows, throwing rainbow patterns on the floorboards.

I sit up a little higher on the couch. "What details have been leaked? You mean about the police investigating suspects?"

She pulls her phone from her purse and flips open the leather cover. "Information like that should not have been released to the press. We still don't know what we're dealing with here, and the last thing I want is public hysteria."

I fiddle absently with the buttons on the remote. "The reporters are saying it's a suspicious death."

"Yeah. I heard."

"Was Colleen murdered?"

"Jenna," she says, "hon, don't ask me that."

I press my lips together. Right. I learned that rule when I came to live with Kate three years ago: Don't ask about police business. Ever.

I moved here when my mom hit the big time with her travel blog, *This Girl's Guide*. Mom was young when she had me. From what I can gather, she was a carefree hippie who apparently didn't believe in contraception, since my dad was just a one-line scribble in her journal. I guess that's why Mom thought I'd be better off with her now-thirty-something-year-old responsible cop sister, Kate. Responsible is good. *Responsible* is not a word I'd ever use to describe my mother.

"Felton," Kate snaps into her phone. Her hazel eyes are trained on the TV screen again. "Are you seeing this Channel Seven report? Vultures."

The muffled voice on the other end of the line—Drew Felton, Kate's partner at the precinct—must be responding with equal outrage, because Kate shakes her head and intermittently says "assholes" or "goddamn bloodsuckers."

I swallow hard. Another rule about living with Kate: when it comes to police-related topics, we're robots. Totally emotionless. We have to be. I can't sit around dwelling over every tragic case that might come Kate's way.

And I was pretty good at being a robot. Until last weekend.

Colleen O'Dell was a Preston Prep girl. We weren't friends exactly, but I knew her. Everyone at Preston knew her.

Kate ends the call and slams her phone down on the kitchen island.

"I've got to go in to the station. We need damage control on this."

I look between Kate and the unmoving, openmouthed reporter on the TV screen.

"I might be home late." She rummages through her purse again and tosses a couple of bills onto the island. "Takeout money, if you need it."

"Thanks." I muster a smile. "Good luck."

As she passes me, she squeezes my shoulder. "I'm sorry

about all this, Jenna. I know you've been relying on takeout a lot this past week."

"And that's a bad thing?"

She quirks an eyebrow. "Well, it's probably not a good thing. Tomorrow night, I'll try to get home before dinnertime, okay?"

"Don't worry," I tell her. "I'm fine." I draw in a deep breath.

She disappears into the hallway, and the door slams shut behind her.

I'm alone now, but I don't un-pause the TV.

Kate doesn't have to say it. I already know.

This is murder.

GARDINERS BAY DAILY PRESS

Saturday, October 6th

Article written by Adrianna Montana

Seventeen-year-old schoolgirl Colleen O'Dell was found unconscious off the coast of Rookwood Beach in the early hours of Saturday, September 29th. Police responded to a report of an unresponsive female and arrived at approximately 6:40 a.m. O'Dell was pronounced dead at the scene.

Following reports of the death, a source who cannot be named for legal reasons said in part, "I saw Colleen fighting with her friend at lunch that day. I don't know what happened after because I went straight to class, but it was intense. Total toxic friendship."

Although Gardiners Bay Police Department declined to comment at this time, it is understood that the death is being investigated and treated as suspicious.

Christine Gordon, the principal at Preston Preparatory School for Girls where O'Dell attended, said, "This is devastating for the Gardiners Bay community. Our thoughts are with Colleen's family, and we hope their privacy can be respected. We will be providing ongoing support for our students during this difficult time."

JENNA: Hollie, please call me. I'm worried about you.

HOLLIE: Did you read the article? Who gave that quote?

JENNA: I have no idea. But it doesn't mean anything. Your name wasn't mentioned.

HOLLIE: What's the difference? Everyone knows it's about me. I'm the toxic friend.

JENNA: Isn't this libel or something? The paper shouldn't be publishing this trash.

HOLLIE: I bet the whole school has read the article by now.

JENNA: You haven't done anything wrong.

HOLLIE: That's not what the press is saying.

JENNA: Please answer my calls. You don't have to go through this alone.

JENNA: Hollie?

JENNA: Meet me at Chai in an hour. Please.

JENNA

When I reach Chai Café, Hollie is seated at one of the deck tables outside. It's a misty October day, but she's wearing sunglasses. She's looking out at the harbor, transfixed by the yachts moored to the jetty that bob endlessly on the water.

I cross the planked deck and slide into the seat opposite her. Hollie's blond curls are pulled into a ponytail, and even with the sunglasses covering most of her face, I can tell from the blush in her cheeks and nose that she's been crying.

"Hey," I say, gently. "Thanks for meeting me. How are you?"

She purses her lips and shrugs. "I ordered for you." She gestures to one of the two tall lattes on the table. The remains of a torn-up sugar packet sit next to her cup.

"Thanks." My strained voice sounds as alien as hers does. Hollie's been my ride or die since I transferred to Preston freshman year. But even before that, Kate and Hollie's mom used to set us up on playdates whenever Mom and I came to visit. When I first moved here, Hollie was the one person aside from Kate who made me feel like I wasn't totally alone. I've always felt like I could tell Hollie anything, like I could talk to her about anything. But now, for the first time in years, I'm completely lost for words.

Hollie breaks our silence. "Was everyone gossiping about me at school yesterday?"

"No." A total lie. "No one even mentioned you."

She runs a hand over her brow, sweeping away stray tendrils of ash-blond hair that have been pulled loose by the ocean breeze. "I don't believe you."

I attempt a smile.

Hollie exhales into the wind. "I just couldn't face school yesterday. I'm so sick of everyone staring at me and whispering. My mom spoke to Principal Gordon about it. She said I could take some time out, but I don't think I can ever go back there." She pauses for a second. "You know this is the first time I've ever ditched?"

I raise my eyebrows, but I'm not exactly surprised. Hollie's a straight-A student, all lined up for valedictorian and future Ivy League prospects. Under normal circumstances, she'd never skip school. But we're not in normal circumstances. I find my voice. "You shouldn't have to cut class. You haven't done anything wrong, Hol."

Her jaw juts out, like she's fighting back her emotions. "That's not what people are saying, though. Have you been on Instagram?"

I bite my lip. "Yeah."

She lowers her voice. "Everyone thinks I killed Colleen, Jenna." She swipes at a tear as it rolls out from beneath her sunglasses.

I reach across the table and squeeze her hand. "No, they don't. No one really thinks you had anything to do with what happened to Colleen." Saying the words aloud sends a shiver over my skin. I wrap my arms around myself, bracing against the ocean breeze.

"That's not true. The police are questioning me."

"I know," I murmur.

"Your aunt came to my house."

I try to keep my voice even, despite the knot that's forming in my stomach. "Kate interviewed you?"

Hollie fiddles with what's left of the sugar packet. "She was really understanding about everything. It was just procedure."

"Yeah, of course. This is Kate's case, so she had to interview you. I'm sure she doesn't think you're guilty, though." Hollie's lips press together, so I quickly add, "Because you're not guilty. Obviously. No one thinks that." I take a sip of coffee, if only to stop myself from talking.

Hollie chews on her thumbnail. "Kate suggested I delete all my social media accounts. She's worried the trolling won't stop, and blocking people isn't working."

"Maybe that's a good idea."

Another tear rolls down her cheek, and I wince. "Or just wait." I change tactics. "Pretty soon everyone's going to realize that what happened to Colleen has nothing to do with you."

Hollie glances around the decked seating area as though she's suddenly remembered that we're not alone. There's tension in her mouth as she eyes the other patrons. Seated at a nearby table, two middle-aged women laugh loudly as they sip at glasses of wine. One of them has a miniature Chihuahua on her lap and holds it tightly as its little muzzle snuffles the table.

Hollie returns her gaze to me. "Colleen..." She hesitates and swallows. "We just had one stupid fight."

Yeah. One very public fight. In the cafeteria, prime time. In a stroke of exceptionally bad timing, Hollie had a huge blowup at Colleen O'Dell the day before Colleen showed up dead. According to Hollie, Colleen had hooked up with some guy that Hollie had been texting. Cue all hell breaking loose in the cafeteria. Throw in an unfortunate "I'll kill you," and bam, we've got ourselves a scandal. Now that the news has broken about Colleen's suspicious death, the story of the cafeteria catfight has spread through Preston like social napalm.

"I heard on the news that Colleen had marks on her throat," Hollie says. "Bruises. Like she was strangled. Is that true?"

I steady my voice. "I'm not sure. I don't remember."

I fight to block the image from my mind, but it slithers its way back, and my stomach turns. The sight of Colleen's lifeless body is tattooed on my memory no matter how much I try to erase it.

"They think I did that?" Hollie murmurs. "People actually think I strangled Colleen?"

"No one thinks that. Come on, you know what the girls at Preston are like. It's just drama. Any sign of a scandal, and they're all over it. Leeches."

"One stupid fight."

I gather my spiraling thoughts. "The heat will come off you. The police will figure this out. It's their job." I think of Kate and the stressed look she's been wearing all week, worry lines creasing her brow and dark circles beneath her eyes. She'll figure this out.

"I hope so, Jenna. I really hope so." Hollie takes a sip of coffee. Her hands tremble around the cup. Her thumbnails are uneven, like she's been gnawing on them for days.

"Just hang in there, okay?"

"I wish I could take back— Oh, perfect." Hollie suddenly shrinks lower in her seat.

I glance over my shoulder as a familiar trio of girls strut onto the café deck. Serena, Brianna, and Imogen. A trifecta of glossy hair, pouty lips, and short skirts. Serena, Hollie, and I used to be a trio, but at some point between the end of junior year and senior homecoming, Imogen and Brianna replaced us. I suspect Serena's elevated popularity has a lot to do with her becoming captain of the cheer squad and dating Max from Rookwood—and subsequently scoring invites to all of the Rooks' parties. Considering Preston is an all-girls' prep school and the Rookwood boys have the whole mysterious bad-boy vibe locked down, having an in with those guys does wonders for one's social ranking. Apparently.

The girls pause when they notice us. They look between each other, as though they're silently debating whether or not to come over to our table. I offer them a halfhearted wave, but the last thing Hollie needs right now is to have to deal with people from school. Brianna and Imogen were among the many people who reposted a now infamous photo of Hollie and Colleen mid cafeteria fight.

The girls start to make their way over.

"Hey," Serena says. She avoids eye contact with Hollie and runs her fingers through her long black hair.

I muster a smile. "Hi."

Hollie says nothing.

"What are you guys doing?" Serena asks. "Just out having coffee?" She nods toward our barely-touched lattes.

"Yep," I say.

"Nice."

There's a beat of silence, and I feel compelled to fill it, if only to patch over the awkwardness. "How about you guys?" I look between them.

"We're going to Rookwood," Brianna jumps in. "There's a cabin party tonight."

My jaw drops a little. "You're kidding, right?"

They frown back at me.

They're not kidding. This explains why they're all so dressed up—super-short minis and low-cut tops, full makeup and teased hair. Brianna's auburn ponytail tumbles over one shoulder, and Imogen's shiny blond hair falls nearly to her elbows.

"You're going to Rookwood? Even after what happened to Colleen?"

Serena waves her hand. "We'll be safe there. We'll be with the guys."

"Yeah," Brianna echoes. "We'll be safe there." Her gaze flickers to Hollie.

Imogen jabs Brianna in the ribs.

The awkward silence is back. The tide sloshes and slaps against the pier.

Serena takes over. "We would invite you... I just don't think it's a good idea for you guys to come tonight. It's still too fresh, y'know?" Clearly, she misunderstands Hollie's and my silence for disappointment, because she carries on quickly, "It's just that there'll be a lot of people there and a lot of them knew Colleen." Her dark eyes skate over Hollie, who's now staring down at her latte. "Not that we think you had anything to do with it, Hol. But people are talking."

I clear my throat. "No problem. Hollie and I have plans anyway." Plans to do anything but go to Rookwood.

There's always a party at Rookwood. I figure the school's groundskeeper is either well versed at turning a blind eye or is totally useless at his job. Serena and her squad always get invited because of her on-off thing with Max. I've tagged along a couple of times, but honestly, I can think of better ways to spend my weekends than getting absolutely annihilated in some abandoned shack.

I summon a smile for Serena. "Have a good time tonight."

"Thanks," she says. "You, too."

At least the trio looks a little guilty before they strut off toward the indoor seating area. But they hardly make it a couple of strides before they lean in close and start whispering with reckless abandon.

"You're being dragged down by association," Hollie murmurs.

I roll my eyes. "You think I'd rather be going to Rookwood with them?"

The girls are in my peripheral. They've found a table, but they're still huddled together in conversation, stealing glances our way.

I try to catch Hollie's straying gaze. "Colleen was always at the Rookwood parties. If she had a bunch of friends there, maybe Serena just doesn't want to antagonize the situation. For you," I add.

"Yeah, right," Hollie mutters. "They're acting like I'm to blame, but any one of them could just as easily have killed Colleen. You know what Colleen was like."

The comment sends a shiver over my skin. Colleen was fun and outgoing, sure, but she had a knack for rubbing people the wrong way. As social as she was, she got a kick out of getting under people's skin. She seemed to know exactly what to say and when to say it, just at the right time to cause optimum damage. Then she'd smile, flip her hair, and strut away from the wreckage.

The sound of Serena's laughter reaches us from across the decking, bringing me back to the present.

Hollie grabs her purse and stands from her seat. "Sorry, Jenna, I've got to go. I can't do this." She steps out from the table.

"Hollie, wait," I call.

But she's halfway across the deck before I can even get up.

Hollie folds her hands together on the picnic table. "So, tell us about this Max guy."

Serena sets her lunch tray down and sighs. "No joke, he's perfect. You know how I always describe my ideal guy?" We nod, and she carries on, "Well, I've found him. For real."

Hollie and I exchange a quick smile. Serena's dated her fair share of "perfect" guys, but I have to hand it to her, something about the way she describes Max seems different. It's only been a week, but I can tell she's already in deep.

Her expression turns dreamy. "He's so sweet. And so hot." She fans out her hands. "I'm talking factor fifty hot."

Hollie arches an eyebrow. "Wow. Factor fifty. Sounds serious."

"Mm-hmm." Serena tilts her head, taking in the spring sunshine.

"We want to meet him," I tell Serena.

"Definitely," Hollie agrees. "We're your best friends. Factor Fifty Guy needs our stamp of approval before this goes any further."

Before you get burned. The words rush through my mind, but I keep my mouth clamped shut.

"There's a party at Rookwood this Friday." Serena's gaze darts between us. "I'm pretty sure I could score us invites."

I wrinkle my nose.

Serena eyeballs me. "What?"

"What?" I echo.

"What's the face for?"

"There's no face."

"Yes, there is," she tells me. "You're doing the face."

"What face?"

"The 'I don't like this plan' face."

I pick at a splinter of wood on the table. "I want to meet Max. Just not at Rookwood."

"Why not?"

"Rookwood isn't exactly my scene."

Serena rolls her eyes. "Jenna, come on. It'll be fun. Max said the Rooks have a cabin in the forest and they hang out there pretty much every weekend."

Hollie sucks in a breath. "Oh, I'm down for a party in the forest." She lifts her soda can and taps it against Serena's.

I frown at Hollie. "Since when is hanging out at Rookwood your idea of a good time?"

She shrugs. "I'm in the mood for something different."

Serena's attention lands back on me. "Jenna, come on. You can't bail on us. We're the three amigos."

"The three musketeers," Hollie adds with a grin.

"The three stooges, more like." I fiddle with the cap on my water bottle. "I don't know. My mom's supposed to call this Friday, and I don't want to miss it."

Serena's brow creases. "So, change the call to Saturday."

"Yeah." Hollie swivels in her seat to face me. "Can't you rearrange the call for another time?"

"No. She's in the middle of nowhere and hasn't had WiFi access in weeks. She'll be passing through a town on Friday, and I'm not sure when she'll have signal again after that." I offer them an apologetic look. "Next time, maybe." It's true about Mom calling, but I'm kind of glad I have an excuse. Partying with the Rooks doesn't sound particularly appealing to me, no matter how curious I am about the "perfect" Max.

"Serena!"

We turn to see a trio of cheerleaders crossing the quad. Imogen, Brianna, and Colleen. Their green-and-white cheer skirts flutter in the spring breeze.

They slide onto the benches at our table and greet Serena with air kisses and shrieks.

I glance at Hollie, and she stifles a laugh.

Ever since Serena joined the cheer squad this year, her teammates have been popping up constantly, as if we had entered a never-ending game of whack-a-mole. Recently, it's gotten even worse since they've gotten wind of her connection to the Rooks. Textbook bad-boy complex.

Brianna leans in and flips her auburn ponytail. "How are things going with Max?" She flutters her eyelashes.

"Amazing," Serena replies, somehow managing to add a couple of extra syllables into the word.

Imogen shakes her head in awe. "I can't believe you're dating a Rook."

The trio squeal, and Hollie and I swap another look.

"You're such a lucky bitch," Colleen drawls, twirling a strand of blond hair around her finger.

Serena smiles back at her with an arrogance that I've never seen on her before. I try to catch her gaze, but she doesn't see me.

"You are, literally, the luckiest," Imogen says. She fiddles with the silver pendant on her necklace, and her blue eyes fix on Serena. "Have you met any of the other guys yet? You have to hook us up with Max's friends."

"Actually, I was just telling Jenna and Hollie that I'm going to try to get us invited to a Rook party this weekend."

Colleen gasps. "I want to go!"

All three cheer girls stare hopefully and expectantly at Serena.

"Let me see what I can do."

Imogen clasps her hands together. "Please. I need this."

Colleen starts tapping quickly on her phone's keypad. "I'm putting us all into a group so we can plan." She reaches across the table and grabs hold of Serena's hand. "Girl," she breathes. "Make it happen. I'll legit die if I can't go to that party."

ADAM

"Friday night never happened. This stays between us."

It's a statement, not a question, but Max's voice wavers on the last word, like he's asking us. Like he's checking with us.

This stays between us?

We're good at that. We're good at closing ranks, at disappearing when we need to and sticking to the shadows when we've got to hide.

Across the dorm room, Max's eyes lock with mine. Tommy is next to him, head down, wild black hair falling over his brow. Tommy's hands are knotted together, and his thumbs are twitching. But Max is still.

He's always still.

Max has crafted his shell into what it needs to be—armor. He doesn't even look like he belongs at Rookwood. He's name-brand, the type of guy advertising agencies use to sell cologne. But Rookwood isn't a cologne ad, it's a cautionary tale. A second chance for kids who happened to catch a judge on a good day.

People around town probably look at Tommy and me and know straight off the bat where we live. Yeah, they're Rooks, for sure. Maybe our hair has grown out too much or our clothes have a couple of holes around the sleeves. Although, sometimes I wonder if when they look at me, on the surface, they think I look just like them. Maybe they don't know I'm a Rook right away. Maybe they don't get close enough to see who I really am. Because I don't let them get close enough. I don't want people to see the guy I see in the mirror, the guy I wish I wasn't.

That's why Max acts the way he does, all shiny on the outside. When the upstanding residents of Gardiners Bay pass him in the street, I swear they think he's one of them. No way they'd guess he got sent to Rookwood for going after his stepdad with a pitchfork.

Max prefers to tell people he's here for hot-wiring a car, because that suits his image better. But I know him. I know how fast he can lose his shit. I've been there. I've been there when he's been scared too.

He's scared now. They both are. Tommy and Max.

I see it in the way Tommy's thumbs won't stop moving. I see it in the way Max's chest is rising and falling faster than usual.

They're both staring at me, waiting for me to speak.

A memory of my old life snakes out from the darkest corners of my mind. Way back when—before Rookwood, before these four walls, before I even knew Max and Tommy existed. Back then, I never would have put my neck on the line for anyone. I had a good life, better than the one I have at Rookwood. I was going places. I had a plan.

But plans don't always work out.

After three years here, I've almost managed to erase my old life completely. My mom's dead, and my last memory of my dad is watching him shrink in the cab's side mirror, the reflection of my scraped-up middle finger giving him and the farm a final farewell.

Now, all the family I need are here at Rookwood. It's just that their blood isn't the same as mine.

Turns out blood isn't thicker than water, after all. All of us here, we're in this together. We'll go down in flames, together, too. A burning inferno. Screaming in the night about the things that came before.

"Yeah," I answer at last. "This stays between us."

She steps into the cabin, and the door slams shut behind her. Maybe the wind caught it from her grasp. Maybe she pushed it too forcefully.

Tommy and I look up from our pool game.

"Hey, Colleen." Tommy's frowning, like he's wondering why she's here. I'm wondering the same thing.

"Hey." She reclines on the couch and stretches out her legs. As far as she's concerned, this cabin is hers now. It doesn't matter that it's on our campus, buried deep in the grounds of Rookwood Boarding School. She's found her place here.

The hunting cabin is a throwback to the days when Rookwood used to be privately owned. Its leather upholstery has faded after so many years, but the old bar with its draft taps still just about works. This place is off the grid, and we've managed to keep it a secret from the staff and the younger boys. For now, at least. But Colleen's going to get us busted if she keeps on showing up like this—her and the other Preston girls. They don't realize how careful we've got to be, sneaking out here after night roll call, picking locks and disabling alarms, and

treading along the halls as though any movement could set off a gre-
nade. Any creaking floorboard or squeaking door at Rookwood could
wake Hank, the night-shift security guard, and a sighting of people
in the forest after dark could lead him straight to our cabin. Then he'd
find all the empty beer bottles and cigarette butts, and they'd tighten
security and have us seniors running laps at dawn every day for a
month to teach us discipline.

But Colleen doesn't care about that. She thinks it's her right to be
here just as much as it is ours.

"Where's Max?" she asks, combing her fingers through her pale-
blond hair.

"I don't know," I tell her. "He's around, somewhere."

"Colleen," Tommy says, "what are you doing here? We're not
having a party tonight. It's just us."

"I know." She strolls to the fridge and peruses the contents. It's
bleak today—a couple of bottles and some leftover pizza. She takes
out a Bud and pops the cap. "I don't want a party tonight, anyway.
I don't want to be around all those Preston bitches. I just want to
chill." She saunters back to the couch and takes a long swig of beer.

Tommy gives me a look across the pool table before bowing down
to take his shot.

She watches us for a while, sometimes talking, sometimes not.
When she's had enough of our silence, she hops up from the couch,
leaving her empty bottle on the coffee table, and skips across the room.
She grabs another beer from the fridge before heading toward the door.

"I'm going to find Max," she says. "No offense, but you guys
are boring as hell."

She disappears back into the night.

"Why is she here?" I ask Tommy. "Has she got something going
on with Max?"

He shrugs. "Beats me."

I frown back at him. "He's still with Serena, though, right?"

"Yeah. As far as I know."

"You think he's seeing Colleen behind Serena's back?"

"Probably."

My eyebrows knit together. "What's wrong with him? Those girls are friends, right?"

"Come on, you know Max isn't serious about Serena. Not like how she is with him…" Tommy trails off as the door swings open and Colleen paces back into the cabin.

Max is trailing behind her. His sun-bleached hair is rumpled. "Colleen," he says. He's breathless. "Just wait. Listen. Please."

JENNA

I don't know what drew me back to Rookwood Beach. A week ago I vowed to myself that I'd never come back here. It's not like Rookwood is on my route home from Chai. Or from anywhere. The cove is tucked away beneath the forested cliff on the other side of the bay, where the silver ocean curls into the rocky shore. And yet, exactly one week after Colleen's body was found, here I am. Back again.

I'm not the only one, either.

There are no police or forensics here now. It's just me and him, just like it was on that morning. The cool wind is moving over him, rippling his faded gray t-shirt and tousling his brown hair.

I slip beneath the railings and jump down onto the beach. Feeling the stones and hard sand under my feet brings me right back to that moment.

The moment that he shouted for help.

He must hear my footsteps above the hiss of the waves

and the groan of the wind because he turns, looking over his shoulder. He tenses, like he didn't want to be found here.

I know the feeling.

"Hi," I say, slowing as I approach. "I didn't mean to scare you."

"You didn't." His voice is husky, kind of scratchy. In this hazy sunlight, his eyes stand out. They're almost an amber tone. Like caramel. He has the whole broad-shouldered jock look nailed down. Six-feet-something, blessed with unfairly nice features, and built like a quarterback. But somehow I can't imagine him fist-bumping guys in the locker room or flirting with cheerleaders. He's quieter than that, more reserved.

Adam dips his head, and his gaze lands on his sneakers. They're damp, spattered with seawater.

"I was just…" He lets the sentence drift off and glances out to the water. The frothy waves slap hard against the rocks before getting sucked back in, stirring the pebbles.

I run my fingers across my brow, pushing back the strands of chestnut hair that have been caught by the gale. "I can't stop thinking about it, either."

He slips his hands into his jeans pockets. We're silent for a moment, kind of entranced by the tide. Then he says, "I couldn't save her."

I turn to him, studying his profile. "It was too late to save her. You didn't have a chance."

His focus comes back to me. "I should have done something."

Somehow his words seem to take on an entity of their own.

"You tried. There was nothing more you could have done for Colleen."

"I could have done something," he murmurs. "I know I could have done something."

I step closer to him and pull him into a hug. I can feel his heart beating. I can feel his breath on my temple. And again, I'm catapulted back to that day. Only now, his clothes are dry, and I'm not shaking. Neither is he.

He takes a sharp breath and pulls away from me. "But it's over now." His eyes are back on the water.

"You're not alone," I tell him. Something about my voice in the howling wind sounds almost haunting. "I was there. I understand how you're feeling."

He bows his head.

"It feels…" I wrap my arms around myself as the gale picks up. "I don't know. Lonely."

He catches my gaze again. "You can always talk to me. If you want. We can swap numbers or something."

The offer dazes me for a second. "Oh. Okay."

Suddenly, there's an unease between us. It's palpable. I hand him my cell, and he adds his contact information before passing it back.

He drags his hands over his face. "I'd better go," he says.

"Yeah. Sure."

He starts to walk away, then stops. "Did you know her?"

"Colleen?"

"Yeah." The wind toys with the strands of his warm-brown hair. "Did you know her?"

"We went to the same school."

"Were you friends?"

"Not really." I cringe at how callous my answer sounds. But it's the truth. Colleen and I weren't friends.

I search his gaze, trying to read his torn expression. "How about you? Did you know Colleen?"

"No," he says. "I didn't."

My heart beats a little faster as I watch him leave. Because I know he's lying.

"I think I like a Rook. Don't judge me."

I squint one eye to scrutinize Hollie. "Continue."

"I got talking to him at the party last night." She pauses. "Speaking of, Miss No-Show, you seem to have recovered from your mysterious illness extraordinarily quickly."

I make a halfhearted attempt at a cough.

Hollie rolls her eyes. "Anyway, I talked to him for like an hour. Maybe more. He was so sweet." She gazes out across the harbor with a dreamy look in her eyes. "I used to think the Rooks were just tough guys with a point to prove, but he was nice. Kind of vulnerable, y'know?"

I raise an index finger. "That's how they hook you in, Hol. It's the whole wounded bird narrative."

She swats me. "He was sweet."

"So, you and this Rook guy, is this going to be Serena and Max, 2.0?"

"Maybe. Colleen says she'll talk to him for me. She's going to give him my number."

"Whoa. Rewind. Are you seriously trusting Colleen O'Dell with your love life?"

"It's unavoidable." Hollie takes a long sip of soda, then shrugs. "She knows the guys. She parties there every weekend. I need an in."

My brow creases. "What about Serena? She knows them."

Hollie shakes her head. "No. Don't tell Serena."

I frown at her over the top of my iced coffee. "Why not?"

"She gets so possessive, like she wants to be the only one who's dating a Rook. I can't deal."

"Okay. Suit yourself. But we both know Colleen's going to screw this up."

She laughs and swats me again.

ADAM

I wait a while before I go back to the beach. I want to be sure Jenna's gone. I can't think clearly when she's around, and I end up doing dumb shit like giving her my phone number. It's not good.

I couldn't think clearly on the morning I found Colleen, either.

The memory of finding her is still raw—I can feel it swimming through me as I retrace my steps.

I look out at the surging ocean. She was right there, tangled, broken. I saw the bruises on her throat. I can't unsee them. I can't unsee her.

I can't un-hear her.

I head toward the shoreline until the pebbles turn to sand. At the water's edge, I take off my sneakers and let my feet sink into the wet sludge where the frothing breakers have spilled across the beach. I'm leaving footprints—heavy, sunken shapes that will be washed away as soon as the next wave comes in.

I toss my t-shirt aside and step into the water. It's cold. Ice-cold. But I keep wading through, letting my limbs turn numb. Before I know it, I'm swimming deeper, slicing through the current with steady strokes. My head aches from the freezing salt water.

It's a while before I let myself stop. I tread through the deep water, and my eyes travel to the forested cliff. It rears high over the ocean, the trees swaying in the bleak autumn wind.

There.

If Colleen had fallen from Rookwood Cliff, she'd have hit the water hard. Probably not hard enough to kill her. But if she wasn't already dead, it would have hurt like hell.

The tide could have pulled her under. But the tide doesn't leave fingermarks.

"Isn't it a little cold for swimming?"

I hear the voice in my mind and suddenly I'm right back there, back with Jenna. Back to the first time I met her.

"Isn't it a little cold for swimming?"

A girl is sitting on a rock and cradling an expensive-looking camera in her lap. The April sunshine catches the red in her long, wavy hair. She smiles at me. The sort of gentle, easy smile that makes me want to smile back.

I'm not usually one to stare, but there's something about this girl. Something that holds my eyes. She's pretty, yeah. Beautiful, even. But it's more than that. She's calm, peaceful. Everything I wish I was.

I wade to the shore and pick up my t-shirt. I'm not used to seeing people out here, especially not this early. "It's okay," I tell the girl. "It's not that cold once you've been out there for a while." I start pat-

ting my skin with my t-shirt, blotting away the salt water before I slip the shirt over my head. "You should try it."

She wraps her arms around herself and smiles. "No, thanks. I like not having hypothermia."

I smile back at her. "Water's better colder. It gets the blood pumping."

"My blood is fine as it is." She crinkles her nose, and I notice the freckles scattered across her cheeks.

I gesture to the camera. "What are you taking pictures of?"

Her sea-green eyes travel to the horizon. "The sunrise."

"Yeah? You get a good shot?"

"I don't know." She lifts the camera, and it beeps as she starts scrolling through her photos. "They're okay, I guess."

"Can I see?"

"Sure. If you want."

I step forward and sit beside her. I'm close to her. Our arms brush together as I lean in to get a look at the screen.

The photos are good. The colors bleed together, oranges and pinks spilling out into a gray world.

"I like this one." I point to an image where the rising sun creates a perfect crescent over the water.

"I like it, too."

The sweet scent of her hair reaches me as the wind flutters the strands.

My heart does something. Just something. There's an attraction. A recognition that I'm here, and this girl is here. I haven't been in that place for a long time.

She turns to me, and I take in the kaleidoscope shades of green in her gaze. "I think it's probably the best one," she says. "The others are out of focus."

"What are you going to do with the picture?"

"I'm trying for an art scholarship."

"For college?"

"Yeah." She tucks a strand of hair behind her ear. *"My art teacher thinks I could have a chance."*

"Hey, if you can get the grades, go for it." The concept is new to me, but it makes me stop for a second. It makes me think.

"Beats having to pay your way in, right?"

"Yeah. What school do you go to?"

"Preston."

I raise an eyebrow. *"The girls' school?"*

"Yes."

"Fancy."

Her cheeks flush, and she breaks eye contact. *"My mom's travel blog took off a few years back. She made enough to cover my tuition."*

The word mom always makes me flinch. Force of habit.

But I carry on. *"Yeah? Lucky you."*

"Mom's pretty much burned through all the money now, though. She's off searching for her next big break."

"Where is she?"

"Vietnam." She quirks an eyebrow. *"For now."*

"You live with your dad?"

"Nope." She starts fiddling absently with a button on the camera. *"I've never met the guy."*

"That sucks. Sorry."

"It's okay. I've been living with my aunt since freshman year. Anyway, I'm going self-sufficient from here on out." She grins at me, and I can't help but mirror it back.

"I hear that."

"You can't rely on anyone but yourself." She presses her lips to-gether, like she regrets saying it. I know that feeling.

So I move on. *"You live around here?"*

"I'm on the other side of the bay, out by Lighthouse Point."

"Nice. You live anywhere near that house where the hedges are all shaped like animals?"

She laughs, and I like the sound. *"The horses? That's my next-door neighbor!"*

"No kidding?"

Another warm smile travels to her eyes. *"How about you?"*

I find myself twisting my wrist, just enough so that she can't see the talon tattoo on my forearm. I don't want to tell her that I'm from Rookwood. As soon as I say it, I won't just be a stranger on the beach to her, I'll be a Rook. Someone to be wary of. Someone to keep away from.

In this moment, I just want to be me. A stranger on the beach.

So, I answer, *"Nearby. Maybe I'll see you around."*

"Probably. My name's Jenna."

"I'm Adam." I stand and push back my wet hair. *"Good to meet you, Jenna."*

"You too, Adam."

By the time I get back to Rookwood, a party has already started up. Through the trees, I can see the cabin. Its grimy windows are a frame into a goldfish bowl. The people inside can't see me, but I can see them. I hear the muffled laughter, the voices, the music. They're all sealed within the walls, caught in a bubble that they can't get out of.

Serena and the Preston girls are here again.

Your friend died, I want to shout. *A girl died, and you still keep coming here.*

Max is with Serena, merged into a tangle of limbs. Her friends are around. One of them is talking to Tommy in the shadows of the back corner. She hands him a bill.

I grit my teeth. I can't go inside.

My car is parked in the glade. I keep it hidden out here in the forest so that the staff don't find it and confiscate it. It's just an old Dodge that someone abandoned in a junkyard last year. When I found it, it was in pretty bad shape. The engine was shot, the brakes didn't work, and it had three busted windows. I spent an entire summer fixing it up, and now it runs like a dream. Well, it runs, anyway.

I slide into the driver's seat. The door gives a groan as I slam it shut.

I start the ignition and listen to the engine rumble in the quiet night. I need a breather from this place every now and then. Tonight's that kind of night.

When I was first sent to Rookwood, they diagnosed me with anger issues. I always knew I didn't have anger issues; I was just mad as hell when I came here. But I'm not mad anymore. People change. Life changes. Doesn't matter to the paper-pushers, though. They still think I've got anger issues. But maybe that's because I've learned how to act to ensure they don't send me back.

I hit the gas and take the freeway, driving until my eyes feel tired. It's the dead of night when I get there.

The farm.

I haven't been back here in a while. I only come when I know he won't see me. Covered by the night. At this hour, no one notices I'm gone and no one notices I'm here. Usually, I pull up on the dirt track and cut my headlights. Then I stay for a while, just watching the crops sway in the darkness.

It's the same here as it always was. The roof still needs repairing, the fencing still needs painting, and the barley shoots still move in the night air. They whisper.

I remember him, and I remember her, back when everything was good. Back when I was a kid, running through the fields, my fingers skimming the golden shoots in the hot sunshine. She'd be laughing, and he'd be working on the porch.

We were happy.

But the memories are scarce. The good ones, anyway. I blocked out the years after he left, when she got thinner and lost control. He showed up here again after she died, acting like this was his place, like he was a parent again.

I know he's in there now, sleeping inside the dark farmhouse. He has someone else in there with him, too. A new wife, and she has a kid. I've seen them playing in the field, just like I used to do. I wonder if they ever talk about me. I wonder if she even knows I exist.

Probably not. I'm just the ghost that haunts his new world. His world without the flaws of the past.

I think of her, my mom.

Then I think of Tommy. My friend. The brotherhood I created when I had nothing left.

My grip tightens around the steering wheel. I start up the engine, and it rumbles, like an earthquake rupturing the calm.

Something bad is coming our way. I can feel it.

But I'm going to stop it.

This time.

JENNA

"Hollie Braithwaite."

I hear her name and freeze. Kate's voice travels into the hallway. She's talking on the phone, and she's using her police-voice, all quick and assertive. I let my fingers slip from the front door, and it closes with a quiet click.

"Yes… Right. But you really think Braithwaite's guilty? Come on, Felton. You really think she's capable?"

I hold my breath, waiting silently for the next snippet of conversation to leak into the hallway.

"But those aren't facts, Felton. It's all hearsay. So, they had an argument? Over, what, some boy they both liked? It's high school stuff."

There's a long pause, and my heart starts beating faster. This proves it. Kate doesn't think Hollie is responsible. Although, by the sound of it, it doesn't seem like Detective Felton is quite so convinced of Hollie's innocence.

"I'd like to take a look at a couple of those statements again.

The ones we took from the Rookwood students. Can you ask Lamar to send those over?"

I focus on not moving a muscle. Not making a single sound.

"The boy who found her, Adam Cole." Kate reels off his name, and I hear papers rustle. "Then let me take another look at Max Grayson and Tommy Drummond. Based on what her friends are saying, Colleen was spending a lot of time with those two boys. Grayson and Drummond are my red flags right now."

Kate ends the call, and I hear the tap of her footsteps heading this way. I snap into action and pace along the corridor toward the kitchen, trying my best to not look totally sketchy.

I breeze into the kitchen. "Hi."

Kate starts. "Oh. Hi, Jenna. I didn't realize you were home."

"Yeah, I just got back. How's it going?" My eyes wander to the paperwork in her hands.

She tucks the documents into a folder, out of sight. "There's a lot going on at the precinct. I need to pull a couple of late shifts. Is that alright with you?"

"Yeah. Of course."

She gives me a sympathetic smile. "Home alone, again."

"Honestly, it's fine. I don't mind." I wait a beat. "Any leads on Colleen's case?"

Kate responds with a sigh. "Nothing concrete yet. I'm sorry." She rests her hand on my arm. "How are you doing?"

"I'm okay. I just want to get to the bottom of this. For Colleen. For Hollie, too."

She breaks eye contact at the mention of Hollie's name.

"You know she didn't do it." The words fall from my mouth before I can stop myself.

Kate purses her lips. She won't say it. At least not to me.

But I need Kate to tell me that Hollie will be fine. That this is all a misunderstanding and my best friend won't get put on trial for murder. For a crime she couldn't possibly have committed.

I know it.

Hollie's not a murderer.

I just hope, for Hollie's sake, that the police never find those text messages.

The summer sun beats down over the boardwalk. Hollie threads her arm through mine as we stroll along the promenade, meandering between the tourists with their beach bags and floppy sunhats. Ahead, the pier extends out over the glistening ocean.

"So," Hollie says, "confirm, yes or no. Movie night at your house tonight, and series binge at mine tomorrow?"

"I can confirm." I finish my popsicle and toss the stick into a trash can on the boardwalk. "Is Serena coming?"

Hollie shrugs. "No idea. I texted her."

"Yeah. Me too." I press my lips together and glance at Hollie. "Should we worry yet?"

Her brow creases. "Worry about what?"

I blow out a tense breath. "I mean, do you think she's okay? It's been over a week, and neither of us has heard from her. That's so not Serena."

Hollie laughs. "She's fine. It's summer break, she's probably spending all her time with her super-hot boyfriend."

"But why isn't she bombarding us with thousands of text messages telling us all about how hot her super-hot boyfriend is?"

Hollie pats my arm. "I'm sure she'll get to that eventually."

"Okay." My gaze wanders to the gently moving ocean beyond the boardwalk railings. "I hope nothing bad has happened to her."

As Hollie and I walk in sync along the warm promenade, I realize what's been bothering me this past week. I miss Serena. I even miss the things that aren't miss-worthy, like waiting an eternity for her to commit to an ice cream flavor. Or her vetoing all of the movies Hollie and I suggest. Who's going to quality control our movie selection tonight?

In so many ways Serena is my polar opposite, but she's my friend. My bossy, impulsive, melodramatic friend. And I miss her.

"Anyway," Hollie says, jolting me out of my sentimental state, "the bigger question is which series we're going to binge. Are we in the mood for intense or lighthearted?" Her arm slips from mine as she scrapes her wild blond curls into a ponytail to trap them from the summer breeze.

I crinkle my nose. "This is going to take some thought—"

"Oh, wait. Cheer girls, ten o'clock." Hollie's arm locks through mine again as she nods in the direction of the pier. Imogen and Brianna are strutting along the planked walkway, heading in our direction. Imogen flutters her fingers in a wave, and Brianna's lips arch into what I presume is supposed to be a smile.

"Hey!" Imogen's silky blond hair swishes behind her as she skips over to us and kisses the air around our cheeks. "What's up, ladies?"

Brianna looks up from her phone long enough to muster another half smile.

"Nothing," Hollie says. "Just wasting time. How about you guys?"

Brianna combs her fingers through her auburn waves. "Same."

"This summer has been so slow," Imogen drawls. "We've literally done nothing."

"Us too." I shift my focus between them. "Have either of you heard from Serena lately?"

They exchange a glance.

"No," Imogen says, leaning in a little closer. "How come?"

All of a sudden, I feel uncomfortable under their prying gazes. Great. The sharks have smelled blood in the water.

"No reason," I say, diverting them from any scent of gossip or scandal. "I guess she's just been spending a lot of time with Max."

Brianna stares at me and slowly chews her gum. "I think she's been hanging out with Colleen."

Hollie chokes out a sound, and her eyebrows shoot up. "Colleen?"

I frown. "I doubt that."

"For real."

Imogen looks blankly at Brianna. "Colleen and Serena? Since when?"

Brianna turns her palms upward, bracelets clunking on her wrists. "Colleen told me she was meeting Serena a couple of days ago."

Imogen blinks back at her with wide blue eyes. "Why weren't we invited?"

"I don't know," Brianna says, jutting out her chin. "Personally, I have no idea why Serena would choose to hang out with Colleen O'Dell over us." Her eyes linger only on Imogen, making it clear that "us" does not extend to Hollie and me. "Colleen is way too extra."

Imogen nods, and her gaze moves to me. "She's too much. And she lies all the time," she adds with an eye roll.

"Tell me about it," Hollie mutters under her breath.

Imogen and Brianna study her, waiting for her to elaborate.

"What, you and Colleen have drama?" Brianna asks.

Hollie's arm tightens around mine. "No. We're good."

I glance at her, but she just smiles and says nothing.

HOLLIE: Serena keeps texting me. I can't deal.

JENNA: About what?

HOLLIE: She's sorry she's been distant lately. Blah, blah, blah.

JENNA: What, you don't buy it?

HOLLIE: Before this, the last time she texted me was July. It's October.

JENNA: So she wants to fix things?

HOLLIE: She just wants the inside scoop, now that she thinks I killed Colleen.

JENNA: Don't say that.

HOLLIE: Sorry. But it's weird, right? What, am I suddenly relevant again?

JENNA: She's our friend, Hol.

HOLLIE: When it suits her. I just don't get her sudden interest.

JENNA: Maybe you should talk to her.

HOLLIE: I can't. You're the only person I trust right now.

ADAM

Serena's here again, at the cabin. She doesn't wait for the parties anymore—she shows up on weekdays now, too. And she comes alone, without her usual squad in tow. Over on the couch, she's wrapped around Max. She won't let him out of her sight.

It's been this way for a while. It's as though the more he pulls away, the tighter she grips. I don't know what hold he has over her, but I get the feeling Serena isn't a girl who likes to lose.

She notices my eyes on her, and she stares back at me over Max's shoulder.

I look away.

Max is in the rec room, watching some trashy family court TV show. Judge Whoever is doling out punishment to some dude who busted his neighbor's mailbox.

I push Max's leg off the couch and sink into the seat beside him.

"You cut class?"

He bites into a strip of licorice, tearing it with his teeth. "Free period."

"Yeah. Same."

His phone buzzes with an incoming text. He glances at it, half smiles, then tosses the phone aside.

I see the name on the message. He's saved the contact as HRG, and the text is all heart emojis and kisses.

"HRG?" I ask.

"Hot Rich Girl."

"Serena?" We met this girl on the pier a couple of weeks back. Max seems into her. He's been bringing her around lately. But he doesn't talk about her much.

"Yup," he says, chewing.

"Does she know you've got her saved as Hot Rich Girl?"

He grins. "Nope."

"She's never seen HRG on your phone?"

He snorts out a laugh.

"What if she sees it? You think she'll be pissed?"

He glances at the TV as the judge bangs the gavel. "Nah. Why would she be?"

"I don't know. Because her name's Serena."

"She'll be fine. It's a compliment. And it's a fact. She's hot, she's rich, and she's a girl."

I look down at the heart emojis again before the phone's screen fades to black. "So, are you serious about her or what?"

"Dude, I've seen her pops cruising around town. He drives a goddamn Bentley." His eyes light up. "She drives a Porsche. Can you believe that shit?"

"Yeah, I can. She's a Preston girl."

He gives a low whistle. "Bank."

I pause. "I wouldn't have had her down as your type."

"What's not to like?"

"I don't know. She seems high-maintenance."

"Yeah, but she's hot. And she's my ticket out of here."

I stare back at him.

"Come on," he scoffs. "Don't tell me you haven't thought about it?"

"What?"

"We graduate this time next year. We'll be out of Rookwood." *He drags his index finger along his throat. "Done."*

"Yeah. And?"

"Contingency plan, bro. What are you going to do after Rookwood?"

My mouth goes dry. "I don't know. Go to college?"

"Who's paying? You?"

"I'll get a job. Rent an apartment somewhere."

He laughs and shakes his head. "Well, good luck to you, man. Enjoy eating from the dumpster while you're sleeping on the streets."

"It won't be like that. I can do stuff."

"Yeah, right! We're nobodies, Adam. Ain't nobody giving us jobs or apartments. Once we're outta here, it's kill or be killed. No way in hell I'm going back home after this."

I force his words from my mind. I don't want them taking root. "What's this got to do with Serena?"

He flicks my forehead. "Catch up. I'm covering my ass with this girl. She told me she's getting some fat inheritance payout as soon as she hits eighteen. She's my meal ticket. Know what I'm saying? She's my nine-to-five."

"That's messed up."

He tears the licorice with his teeth and grins. "Kill or be killed."

JENNA

I hold my phone close to my ear as I try to think of something to say. Something remotely positive. Something that doesn't involve Colleen or her case. "I missed you at school today, Hol. We had to play dodgeball in gym, and I had no one to share my trauma with."

Hollie offers an empty laugh. "Sadists. I'm glad I ditched if dodgeball's the best they could come up with."

"I know, right? I feel like I should put in a formal complaint. I swear, I have a bruise on my butt now."

"Brutal."

She's still Hollie, but she's not the Hollie she was a few weeks ago, before this witch hunt started. It's as if she's just going through the motions, responding when she's supposed to respond, laughing when she's supposed to laugh. But it's hollow. She's a shell.

"Mr. Waller said he'd email you the English assignment. Did you get it?"

She sighs. "I don't know. I haven't checked."

"I think you can still make the grades for valedictorian, as long as you send the homework in on time."

She makes a vaguely disinterested noise, and my stomach tightens.

I take a deep breath. "So, I was thinking you should come over to my house tonight. We can watch movies, pick up Chinese food from that takeout place in town—"

"I can't," she says softly.

"Well, I could come to you. If your mom doesn't mind?"

"I'm supposed to go into the station for more questioning tomorrow. I should probably rest up."

"Hollie," I murmur. "Come on. Don't shut me out. I'm here for you, okay? This is just a blip. We'll get through it, together." My gaze wanders to my bedroom window, where the maple branches are swaying outside.

She's quiet again.

"I'm so sorry you're going through this, Hollie."

"Yeah." Her voice wavers. "I know you are."

"Everyone misses you at school." I move on, fumbling over my words. "It's not the same without you."

"What, people actually want the murderer back?" she jokes. But it falls flat.

"No one thinks you did it. Not really." Even as I say it, I can't be entirely sure that the statement is true.

Silence.

"Hollie, please let me come over. I'll keep you company. I'll—"

"Sorry, Jenna. I've gotta go. My mom's calling me."

I didn't hear Mrs. Braithwaite in the background. All I heard was the crack in Hollie's voice when she told the lie.

But I don't challenge her. "Okay. I'll call you tomorrow. I hope everything goes well, you know, with the…"

"Thanks," she murmurs.

When I end the call, there's a painful tightness in my chest. Hollie shouldn't be punished like this. She would never have hurt Colleen. I know that. And so should all the piranhas. There was just one stupid fight—over a guy.

There's a knock on my bedroom door.

"Come in," I call.

My door creaks open, and Kate peers around it. "Can we talk?"

I smile, but it feels like more of a grimace. "Sounds ominous."

She steps into the room and perches on the edge of my bed. "There's no easy way to say this." She takes a breath. "I have some bad news."

My grip tightens around my phone. "Okay."

She rests her hand on my leg. "Jenna, some text message transcripts have been handed in as evidence in Colleen's case. A message was sent from Hollie's number on the night Colleen died."

My stomach does flips. This is what I was afraid of.

BRIANNA: Guys, what the hell just happened?

COLLEEN: I don't know, Bri. Hol, want to explain why you lost it with me at lunch?

COLLEEN: No response? Typical Hollie. No backbone.

IMOGEN: What did you do, Colleen?

COLLEEN: Nothing! Why do you assume it's my fault?

SERENA: Have you guys been online? Loads of girls are posting pictures of Colleen and Hollie fighting in the cafeteria!

IMOGEN: Oh my god. Just ignore it.

COLLEEN: I'm glad people documented it. They're only posting proof of me being attacked by her. Unprovoked! She's not even sorry. I might delete her from our group.

JENNA: Can we stop texting about this, please?

COLLEEN: No.

COLLEEN: Texting, texting, texting.

COLLEEN: I'll keep going until she answers us or removes herself from MY group. Girl, bye. No one even likes you anyway, Hol.

HOLLIE: Get over yourself, Colleen. You're the one that none of us like. Do us all a favor and go kill yourself.

Hollie has left the group.

ADAM

"The cops were here again." Tommy shuts the door to our room and leans against it. "They questioned me, and I think they questioned Max too. I saw him coming out of Lomax's office."

I sit up a little straighter on my bed. "Yeah? What did they ask you?"

He runs a hand through his shaggy black hair. "They asked how I knew Colleen. If I think anyone might have had it in for her, that kind of thing."

"Why were they asking you?"

"Because they know something." He drags his hands over his face and groans.

"Don't worry." I tug at my collar. It feels tighter, all of a sudden. "Her friends probably said she'd been hanging out with you, that's all. They have to follow any leads. They're covering all their bases."

He bangs the back of his head against the door. "We're screwed."

"What did you tell the cops?" I ask.

"That Max is dating her friend Serena. That's it."

"Good. Just act normal. Be you."

"Yeah, right," he mutters. "Being me is what got me sent here in the first place."

I squint at him. "No, getting busted with narcotics is what got you sent here."

He grimaces.

"Alright," I say, "so act squeaky clean. Act like Max."

"We're going down for this," Tommy says. "We'll be their scapegoats. I know it."

"No, we won't." I slap my hands together. "We just have to sail through this investigation, then we can move on with our lives. We've got our futures to think of."

"What futures?" he mutters.

"I don't know. College? Whatever comes after that?"

Something close to a laugh escapes him. "College? Since when are we going to college?"

I shrug. "It's possible, right? Second chances and all that."

He shakes his head. "Rookwood was our second chance, Adam. Guys like us don't get a third."

I tap on the door with my knuckles.

Through the glass partition, I see Principal Lomax look up from her paperwork. She takes off her glasses and beckons me into her office.

"Hi, Adam," she says. "What can I do for you?"

Suddenly, I feel warm. Too warm. "I wanted to talk to you. About my future." I press my palms together.

"Well, sure. Take a seat." She gestures to the chair opposite her.

I sit and trace my thumb along the uneven ridge of the oak desk. It's a while before I realize I haven't spoken.

"Adam?"

I clear my throat. "Yeah. I wanted to talk to you about scholarships."

She folds her hands together on the desktop. "Okay."

"Would I be eligible for something like that?"

"A scholarship?"

"Yeah." I hold my breath while I wait for her answer. No. She's going to say no. I can feel it.

"Well, I'll have to take a look at your GPA, but I know you've got a good track record with your grades. No promises, but it's certainly something we can shoot for."

Relief floods through me. For the first time in years, I see a chance. Possibilities.

"What kind of scholarship would you like to aim for?" She takes a pen from the crammed pot on her desk and reaches for a notepad.

"I don't know. I'm pretty good at math, I think?"

She jots something on the pad. "Yes, you are. You're a great student." She pauses, assessing me with her gaze. "What are your aspirations, Adam?"

I rub the nape of my neck. "I don't know. I didn't think college was in the cards for me because of the money. But I could go on a grant, right?"

She nods, encouragingly. "Absolutely."

"I've been thinking about studying law. I already understand how the system works. I really think I could make something of myself. I think I could turn things around."

Her eyes crinkle into a smile. "That's why you're at Rookwood, Adam. It's never too late to turn your life around."

ADAM: Tommy said cops were in Lomax's office today. Did they call you in?

MAX: Yeah. What did T tell them?

ADAM: Nothing.

MAX: Did he drop my name?

ADAM: No. Of course not.

MAX: Good. Better not.

ADAM: Do you know why the cops wanted to talk to you again? Tommy's worried a second round of questioning means they're closing in on us.

MAX: You and T need to chill. They're grasping at straws, and they can't pin this on us without proof. Tell T to keep his mouth shut. I don't need him screwing this up for all of us.

ADAM

It's never too late to turn your life around. That's what I keep telling myself.

But the walls are closing in. I loosen my collar. This dorm room is stifling, and the air feels thin. It's always dark in here, no matter how light it is outside.

I pull my phone free from the charging cable and type out a message to Jenna. It has to end here. The lying. I can't do it anymore. I'll tell her everything. Right from the start.

My fingers move fast over the keypad, spilling my worst words into the message box. Then I toss my phone onto the bed and ball my hands. Because I'm not going to send that message.

Because it's not just me anymore. It's not my truth to tell.

"Your shot."

Max's voice brings my attention back to the cabin. I lift my cue and take my turn. The red ball sinks into the pool table's pocket.

Max leans against his cue. "Okay, bud. I've got a good one—"

"Hold up. I made the shot!" I point to the corner pocket.

"Doesn't matter. I still get to ask a question. That's the game."

"I thought the game was Truth if you miss a shot?"

"It was." Max grins and takes a swig of beer. "But I changed the rules."

I glance at Tommy, and he shrugs back at me.

"Alright," I say to Max. "Hit me."

He taps his cue on the floorboards. "What's the worst thing you've ever done?"

My jaw clenches.

"And don't bullshit me," he adds. "I'm talking, the shadiest shit you ever pulled. The shit you get nightmares about."

I lift my beer and knock some back. "I don't know. I busted my dad's Jeep when I was a kid."

Max snorts. "Nope."

"What?"

"You're trying to tell me that's the worst thing you've ever done?"

"It was a nice Jeep."

Max shakes his head. "You're full of shit."

"For real. I can't remember anything else." I don't look at Tommy because I know he knows I'm lying. "You're up," I tell Max, and I gesture to the table with my cue.

Max takes his shot. He's sloppy now. The ball bounces off the pocket and ricochets across the table. He cusses under his breath.

"Okay, same to you," I say. "Worst thing you've ever done?"

Max looks up from the game and meets my eyes. "I killed a guy." There's a beat of silence before his face dissolves into a smile. "Hey, if you can lie, I can lie too."

"I wasn't lying."

"Neither was I."

"*Whatever.*" I hand my cue to Tommy. He lines up his shot and sinks a ball.

"*Okay, I got another one,*" Max says. "*If you had to.*" He aims his beer bottle at Tommy. "*If you really had to choose, who'd you go for: the hot tattooed girl who works at the market or the cougar from the bus station?*"

Tommy stares down at the table. "*I don't know. Neither.*"

Max splutters and sloshes beer onto the floor. "*Neither? You're lying.*"

"*Neither of them are my type.*"

His jaw drops. "*Not your type? Come on.*"

Tommy sighs, and I look at him. "*Fine, hot tattooed girl.*"

Max reaches across the table and slaps him with a high five. "*You're damn right it's hot tattooed girl.*" He stoops low to take his shot, then cusses again when he misses the pocket.

Tommy catches his gaze. "*Straight up,*" he says to Max, "*are you as into Serena as she's into you?*"

Max smirks.

"*So, that's a no,*" Tommy says.

"*What about the other girl you've been texting, then?*" I ask.

Max's head snaps up. "*What?*"

"*You've been texting someone else,*" I keep going. "*You're always on your phone, and I don't think it's to HRG.*"

He mumbles a response.

His twitchy expression makes me laugh. "*So I'm right? What, are you in love with this other girl or something?*"

He won't meet my eyes. "*What kind of a dumbass question is that?*" he mutters.

Tommy and I swap a glance.

I nudge Max with my pool cue. "*Who is she?*"

"Whatever, bro."

I shake my head and line up my next shot.

We keep playing. We keep drinking. We keep going until everything starts to blur.

Tommy is the first to bail. It must be nearly two a.m. by the time he heads back to the dorm. It's always better to sneak back in while it's still dark. There's less chance of getting caught by night security when the on-duty guard is tired and getting sloppy. But Max and I aren't done yet. Now it's just the two of us.

"I don't love Serena." The admission springs out of nowhere. His eyes are unfocused.

"I know," I tell him.

"Yeah."

"But there's someone else?" I can hear the slur in my own voice now. We've drunk too much, both of us.

Max looks at me. He doesn't answer.

"So, why are you still with Serena?"

"I like her. She's cool."

"Because she's got money?"

"No. It's not just that." He lowers his gaze and runs a hand across his mouth. "But I need her. I need her to get me out of here." His words are quick, urgent. "You know I can't go back. My life, my family, stealing cars and dealing, just to get by from one meal to the next. Everything before. I can't go back to that life."

I stay quiet.

"They're in over their heads," he says. "My folks, my brother... Full-on addicts, man. I can't go back to that life."

"I get it."

He rubs the back of his neck. "I've moved on from that. I figure I was lucky to get out once. I might not be so lucky a second time."

"But using Serena like this? You know that's not the way. She loves you."

His jaw tenses. "And I like her. I told you that. Look, you don't understand what my life was like before Rookwood. You don't know."

"Yeah, I do."

"What, your family's screwed too?"

I don't answer. I keep playing. I keep drinking.

It's a while before the words fall from my mouth. "You know what I said earlier?" My voice sounds fuzzy.

"What?" Max asks. His voice is different too. Slower. Thicker.

"When I told you about my dad's Jeep."

"Yeah."

"That's not the worst thing I've ever done."

JENNA

The upstairs of Kate's house mirrors the décor of downstairs: pale tones, large windows, and heaps of light and airy space. The walls are painted in soft pastels, and the furniture is minimalistic. In fact, my bedroom is probably the only room in the whole house that shows any sign of bold colors and clutter—and that's only because Kate finally let me decorate after I'd been here almost an entire year. I guess that's when we both realized my visit wasn't temporary.

I push the cushions aside and sink onto my bed with my phone.

Did you show the police the messages in our group chat? I type to Serena. The ones after Hollie's fight with Colleen?

My phone pings with an incoming message.

No. Of course not.

I toss my cell aside. Hollie deleted that message after the news broke of Colleen's death, so either someone from our group sent a screenshot to the police or the thread was recovered from Hollie's or Colleen's records somehow.

But Hollie didn't mean anything by her message. She was just mad.

I reach for my phone again and open Colleen's private Instagram page. She has a public one too, but she set up this locked burner account under a fake name, probably so that her parents wouldn't find out about what she'd been doing most nights when they thought she was asleep in bed. Row after row of pouty selfies stare back at me. There are a couple of group shots too, where Colleen has her arm draped around Preston girls or Rookwood boys. Her makeup looks a little smeared, and her eyes are unfocused, like she's had a long, beer-fueled night.

Many long, beer-fueled nights.

Even if Kate is bound by law to keep the case details private, there's no reason why I can't do a little investigating of my own. Hollie always had my back when I was the new kid at Preston, the kid who didn't have a flashy car or the most on-trend designer clothes. Now it's my turn to repay the favor.

Hollie's in trouble, and she needs me. She's falling to pieces, and I can't just abandon her. I won't.

I isolate the most recent picture in Colleen's gallery. It was posted a little over a week ago, on Friday, the last time she was seen alive. I enlarge the thumbnail. It's a selfie of Colleen, posing with her face screwed up, tongue lolling out and her pinkie and index finger raised. It was taken at the Rookwood cabin; I recognize the log walls and hunter-green leather sofa. There are two people in the background. They're not directly *with* Colleen, but they're there.

I recognize one of them right away.

Adam.

He's nearly out of the frame, standing next to the pool table with a cue in his hand. The muscles in his arm look taut beneath his t-shirt, like he's tense. Brown hair is curling onto his brow, and his golden eyes are fixed on Colleen.

I knew it. I've seen this photo before—it showed up on my feed right after it was posted. This confirms it. Adam knew Colleen. More than that, he was with her on the night she died.

I leave Colleen's page and type *Adam Cole* into the search bar. His face pops up at the top of my results. There isn't much on his profile: just a few pictures of him with some of the other Rooks. I enlarge one shot of Adam with two other guys. I recognize Max, Serena's boyfriend, with his sun-kissed hair and perfect smile. There's another familiar face in the picture too—the same guy who was caught in the background of Colleen's last selfie. All three boys stare back at me, grinning out from their frozen world.

I click the image so that their tagged names appear.

Adam Cole, Max Grayson, and Tommy Drummond.

Tommy. The boy with dark, scruffy hair and sunken shadows beneath his eyes.

That's him. All three people mentioned by Kate just so happen to be pictured together.

Before I lose my nerve, I type a new message on my phone and hit send.

ADAM

It's dark by the time I notice her message.

Hey, Adam. Can we meet?—Jenna.

Just seeing her name makes my heart thump harder in my chest. It's funny, but despite the impact she's made on me, I barely remember her being there that day. She's merged with the memory of tangled fishing net and seaweed wrapped around Colleen O'Dell's body. Just thinking about it, I can almost feel the light of dawn stinging my eyes, still bleary from the alcohol I'd consumed in the hours before. I can almost feel the weight of her lifeless body in my arms and the tide pulling at my shins.

It was a dumb move giving Jenna my number. I still don't know why I did. Maybe I was caught up in the moment. Or it could have been the way she looked at me like I was honest. The way she made me feel like I wasn't drowning.

I stare at my phone, fumbling for something to say back to her.

I could spew some long-ass response, asking why she wants to meet, pretending like I don't already know. But I just type back, Yeah. Where?

Rookwood Beach? I can come now, if you're free?

Yeah. I'm free.

I get up from the couch. I'd almost managed to mute the sounds of the party starting up around me. But as soon as I move, I'm back in the room. Music, voices, white noise, and thick, smoky air. The cabin is big enough to hold a party but small enough and deep enough into the forest to not look suspicious to the Rookwood groundskeeper. Tommy, Max, and I found it last year, covered in climbing ivy and buried in the evergreens that envelop the school. It had probably been nice back in its day, all oak paneling and expensive looking, like Rookwood was before the school took it over. I figure after the estate was abandoned, the hunting cabin was left to ruin. It was ours for the taking, because no one else wanted it. Like us. The cabin was just another Rook.

Tommy looks up from the couch, black hair falling into his eyes. "Where are you going?"

"Out. I'll be back."

He doesn't need more than that. If he knew I was meeting a Preston girl, he'd probably try to stop me. I can read his body language: he's on edge. He looks around, noticing Max across the room. Serena's curtain of dark hair covers

Max's face; she's on his lap, kissing him, marking her territory. Her friends are around too, playing beer pong with some of the guys.

I leave the cabin and step into the night. No one else asks where I'm going.

I jog through the shadowy forest, knowing exactly how to navigate the uneven ground from years of practice. I head downhill along a rough path toward the shore. The air is cold, colder than it has been in months.

As the path levels, the dirt underfoot gives way to pebbles. Ahead, the moonlight reflects off the water. She's there, standing on the shoreline, looking out at the inky ocean. The water has mostly disappeared in the darkness, but its constant hiss and crash is still there.

She turns, and the breeze moves through her hair.

I pick up my pace. "Hey."

"Hi. Thanks for coming." The wind carries the scent of her sugary shampoo to me, but she keeps her distance.

She's guarded with me now, not like she was when we saw each other before. The compassion in her voice is gone.

"You said you didn't know Colleen." She jumps straight into it.

It stuns me for a second.

"Is that true?" she asks.

"Yeah." I stuff my hands into my jacket pockets.

"I don't believe you."

I hesitate, glad that the surging ocean buffers the silence.

She holds up her phone, and I'm momentarily blinded by the bright screen light. It's a picture of Colleen at the cabin.

"This was the last night Colleen was seen alive," she says. Her eyes are focused on me, and her mouth is tight.

My gut twists at the sharpness of her tone. It shouldn't be like this, not with her. I look into her eyes, trying not to break.

"You knew Colleen." The mistrust in her voice is like a knife through my rib cage.

I steel myself, bracing for what's coming.

Her fingers move quickly over her phone's screen, and the next thing I know, she's zoomed in on me. In the picture, I'm staring at Colleen.

"I didn't know her well," I mutter.

"She came to your parties a lot."

"A lot of people come to our parties a lot."

"You're looking right at her in the picture." She angles her phone to my line of vision.

"I see that. Doesn't mean I remember it."

She slips her phone into her messenger bag and folds her arms across her chest. "If you know anything," she prompts, "anything at all…"

"I don't."

"My friend Hollie is going through hell right now. Everyone thinks she had something to do with Colleen's death. Even the police are looking at her."

"Maybe she did it."

Her lips press together. "She didn't. I know she didn't."

"How do you know?"

"Because I know Hollie. She's not a killer."

I draw in a breath and say nothing.

"Colleen was at Rookwood on the night she disappeared."

I keep my voice even. "I see that."

"Do you know anything?" She clasps her hands together, pleading. "Did you see anything?"

I swallow hard. "I don't remember her being there."

"Maybe we're not friends," she says, "me and you. I get that. I get that you don't need to tell me anything. You don't owe me anything. But, that day, the day that you found Colleen, we went through that together."

I look down at the dark pebbles.

"I saw it, Adam," she carries on. "I saw how desperately you tried to save her. She was murdered, and there needs to be justice. I know you know that too."

"Yeah. I do."

"Earlier you said there was more you could have done. What did you mean by that?" She reaches out and touches my hand. Her fingers fold around mine, and I let my thumb rest on hers, feeling her cool skin beneath mine.

My heart thumps hard in my chest. "I don't know. Maybe if I'd found her sooner..."

Her fingers slip from mine, and she rubs her hand over her eyes.

"Maybe if I'd gotten to her faster..."

"Okay," she says at last. She believes me. The unwavering resolve she'd had a few minutes ago is starting to crumble. She's backtracking now. "Okay. I just thought maybe..."

"Maybe what?" I press.

"I thought maybe you knew something."

"I don't." The words fall out so easily, it almost surprises me.

She's searching my eyes in the moonlight, and I fight the urge to look away. I hate myself for doing this to her.

"Who's Tommy Drummond?"

"Tommy?" My stomach drops at the mention of his name. "One of the guys at Rookwood. Why?"

"I've heard his name, that's all."

"Yeah? From who?"

She shrugs.

My mind is racing, the thoughts coming too fast for me to catch. "I should go," I tell her. My voice sounds hoarse, rough from the salty air. "I'm sorry I can't help your friend."

She doesn't respond.

"Tommy. What are you doing, man? It's the middle of the night."

He's out of bed. A lanky silhouette in the darkness of our room. He's pulling off his bedsheets, bunching them into a ball. "Nothing. I just spilled some water."

I sit upright.

"Oh. You okay?" I ask.

"Go back to sleep." He doesn't look at me. He's trying to get the standard-issue blue cover off his duvet, fiddling clumsily with the buttons.

"You need some help?"

"No. It's fine. Just go back to sleep, Adam. I'm going to do a load of laundry before any of the guys wake up."

"The laundry room is locked. Hank always closes up after lights out."

There's moonlight leaking in through the thin curtains, and I watch him.

I don't know at what point Tommy and I became friends. It happened over time, without me even realizing it. When you share a bedroom with someone for 365 days out of the year, your lives start merging without you even noticing. After a couple hundred days, you realize that you know more about each other than you know about anyone else. You start keeping each other's secrets as well as you keep your own.

Tommy kicks the low bed frame. "Damn it," he mutters. The bundle of sheets drops from his arms and tumbles onto the floorboards.

I heave myself out of bed. "It's okay. The lock is easy to pick. I had to go in there one time when I left my clothes in one of the dryers."

I help him gather the sheets, and we tread carefully from our room. The halls are dark, with a couple of night-lights plugged into the walls to spotlight a path. Health and safety precautions, probably. We walk in silence, and I jimmy open the laundry room door with a paper clip.

Tommy flips the light switch, and suddenly everything is painfully bright. I wait on the edge of the room while he fills the washing machine and pours in a whole lot of detergent.

I don't say anything. He doesn't either.

As we pad back to our room, I think about asking him if he wants to talk about it. But I lose my nerve. It's not my business to know what's going on in his head. It's just my secret to keep now.

I'll never tell anyone about tonight. Or about any of the other nights. Tommy doesn't ask me not to tell the others. He doesn't have to.

He won't tell them any of my stuff, either. Like the time he walked in on me bawling my eyes out in the dorm after a call with my dad. I told Tommy about my mom that day, and he helped me drag the wardrobe six inches to the left to cover the hole I punched through the plasterboard.

He never breathed a word. I know he didn't.

Because Tommy's pretty damn good at keeping secrets.

But then, so am I.

To: STUDENTS
From: PRESTON PREPARATORY SCHOOL
Subject: Memorial Reminder.

To all students,
Following the tragic passing of senior Colleen O'Dell, we will be holding a memorial in the Main Hall at 12:30 p.m. this afternoon, Monday, October 8th. All classes will be canceled today, to resume as normal on Tuesday, October 9th. As was the case last week, our grief counselor, Dr. Emily Patterson, will be on site and taking appointments between the hours of 9:00 a.m. and 3:00 p.m. Please contact Reception ex 201 to reserve a slot.
As mentioned in my preliminary email last week, today will be a chance for all students, parents, staff, and alumni to join together in memory of our friend Colleen.

Kind regards,
Christine Gordon
Principal at Preston Preparatory School for Girls

JENNA

Sunlight streams through my bedroom window on Monday morning, waking me before my alarm. I fumble around my nightstand for my phone. An email from Preston flashes across the screen.

My eyelids are still heavy from sleep—or lack of sleep, more accurately. I spent most of the night tossing and turning, my mind racing with warped images of Colleen.

I'd completely forgotten about the memorial. A notification from Preston about canceled classes would have normally meant a celebratory extra couple of hours in bed. But the last thing I want is to go back to sleep and continue whatever messed-up nightmares my subconscious is brewing. Besides, nothing about today feels celebratory.

I need a distraction. Focusing on my portfolio seems like a good place to start. I've been avoiding it for a while. Ever since we found Colleen, I haven't been able to bring myself to look through the photos I'd taken that morning.

Grabbing my camera from the dresser, I make my way

downstairs, then through the bifold doors and out into the garden. Tucked away in the backyard, there's a bench beneath a maple tree. I brush the fallen leaves away and curl up on the seat. A sparrow hovers at Kate's bird feeder, jabbing its beak at the mesh covering the seeds.

I raise my camera and focus on the bird.

Mom loves this kind of nature shot. She used to say her favorite part about visiting Kate was watching the birds. I remember thinking that was kind of a weird comment to make, as though spending time with her sister wasn't the main event. But I understand it now. Mom's life has always been fast-paced, always in a cloud of smog and chaos. I guess she liked to stop sometimes. Maybe, back then, she was envious of the birds because they were allowed to fly away.

My camera was the first thing Mom bought me after her blog took off. She got a fat cheque from some glossy magazine that wanted to publish her articles, and she took me straight to the electronics store. "Jenna," she said as the cashier rang up our bill, "every time you pick up this camera, I want you to remember how even the smallest of details play a role in the big picture. Capture every detail, no matter how small it seems."

Looking at the camera now, with its fancy high-speed autofocus, dual pixel sensor, and smooth leather strap, I feel like it's the most tangible memory I have left of Mom. The rest seemed to dissipate after she left.

At least with this camera, I have a way of being relevant in her life. We can send each other pictures, snapshots of lives that no longer interweave.

I tuck my legs underneath me and brace myself to look

through the photos. They're mostly scenery shots or beach landscapes, contenders for my portfolio. Everything is safe, familiar.

But as I venture a little further back in the library, the images change. The tones and hues get darker. There are people in the frames: Hollie, Serena, Imogen, Brianna...

My breath catches. These photos are from the cabin at Rookwood. I barely remember being at this party, let alone taking these pictures. The time stamp on the images dates them back to early summer, around the time Serena first started dating Max. This was back when being invited to Rookwood was supposed to be some coveted honor that we couldn't pass up on. It only took two cabin parties for the novelty of being invited to wear off for me. They were just alcohol-fueled binges, with people hooking up in dark corners or passed out on the floor.

As I swipe through the pictures, I try to remember faces, conversations, anything that'll remind me that I was more than just the person behind the lens. I stop on one photo and zoom in.

Scattered memories come flooding back to me.

It's Adam.

He's not just someone in the background this time. This is a photo of *him*. He's staring straight ahead, his honey-colored eyes focused, but not on the camera. His expression is saying so much, it's a real emotion—wistfulness, hopelessness maybe. I'd seen something private, and I'd stolen it.

A shiver skates over me, and I force myself to move on.

There are shots of Colleen, too. Mostly, she's posing for the camera, blond hair flipped to an exaggerated side part. Just like in her Instagram posts, her makeup is smudged and her sky-blue eyes are bloodshot. It dawns on me that I didn't really know Colleen other than *this*—this picture, this persona, the party girl looking for attention. Same with the Rooks, their hard-edged personas are all they show. But there's so much more beneath the surface. It makes me think of my other pictures, the sparrow whose wings move so fast it's almost impossible to see anything beyond a blur, but then the still-frame captures a moment, exposing every silken feather and hidden color. Or the ocean, where the close-up shots capture glimpses of seaweed, rocks, or fish living beneath the gently rippling surface.

There's so much more to see in the smaller details. I just need to look a little closer.

I know it.

ADAM

"Take my picture!"

My eyes travel across the room to where Colleen is standing, sway-ing, pouting, and posing with one hand on her hip.

"Jenna!" she yells again. "Take my picture."

The girl lifts her camera and holds it steady as she focuses the lens on Colleen.

I can't tell if she's recognized me from that dawn on the beach. I rec-ognize her, though. Long chestnut-brown hair, sea-green eyes, calmly watching the world pass by behind the safety of the camera's lens.

Colleen adjusts her pose, and Jenna takes another shot.

Colleen's wasted. They've only just arrived, and she's already struggling to stand upright without losing her balance.

I know what comes next. With each hour, she'll get a little drunker, a little looser. She'll get closer to the guys. To Max. And he'll let her.

I don't think Max cares. He likes the attention. Yeah, Serena gives him attention. But what's the harm in getting more? He keeps telling me that Colleen is just a friend. It's no big deal.

I don't think Serena would see it that way.

Colleen stumbles off across the cabin, wobbling on her high-heeled shoes and sloshing her drink over the rim of her cup.

My eyes land on Jenna.

She frowns for a second, like she's trying to figure out where she knows me from. Then she smiles.

She knows who I am. Busted. One of the boys from Rookwood. One of the Rooks.

I stand and make my way across the crowded room, heading toward her.

She looks up at me from her spot on the couch. "Hey. I thought you looked familiar."

"Yeah. You, too." I gesture to the empty spot next to her. "Is anyone sitting here?"

"No. It's free." She shuffles over to make room for me.

I sit beside her, and just like that I'm right back on the beach with her. Same girl, same camera, same graze of our arms. Only now, we're not alone. And our soundtrack is the cacophony of voices and music, instead of the rush and crash of the ocean hitting the pebbled shore.

"You guys are friends?" I direct my beer bottle to where Colleen is climbing onto the pool table. Her skirt is riding up her thighs. I look away.

"We go to school together."

Got it. "How's your scholarship portfolio coming along?"

"I think I managed to get some good shots." She smiles again, and I swear my heart does an extra beat.

"So, what's next?" I nod to the camera tucked beside her. "What's your latest subject?"

"People," she says. "People and their everyday lives."

My focus strays to the pool table. "Like that girl?"

She laughs. "No, not Colleen and her drunken escapades. I'm more interested in the people who don't know they're interesting."

"Oh, yeah?"

"Like you."

I feel warm, suddenly. "You think I'm interesting?"

"Yeah. Mysterious, early-morning beach dweller. You never mentioned you were from Rookwood."

I half smile. "Can you blame me?"

She frowns, waiting for me to explain.

"I didn't want you to judge me," I say.

"Fair point. I wasn't exactly jumping to tell you that I go to Preston."

I tilt my head. "Why not?"

"Same reason."

"I wouldn't have judged you." I pause. "That much."

She grins. "I wouldn't have judged you that much, either."

"Just a little."

She pinches her thumb and forefinger together. "A little."

But her words don't make me feel like I'm being judged. Not even a little.

Her gaze wanders over my face. "So, you live here, at Rookwood?"

"Yeah."

"What's that like?"

The question catches me off guard. People don't usually ask a question like that so bluntly—not about Rookwood. They dance around it, pretend like it's normal.

"It's not so bad."

"I thought this place was supposed to be super strict. How come you get to have parties out here every weekend?"

I lean back against the sofa cushions. "Believe me, it's not that *simple. Coming out here without getting caught is a major pain in the ass. But it's our sanctuary, so it's worth it."*

"Ah, I see." Her eyes linger on mine. "You all seem pretty tight. The boys who go here, I mean."

I glance across the room. Tommy and Scotch have bailed on their pool game because Colleen is on the table, dancing to the thrum of the sound system. Her blond hair is swaying around her shoulders. Max is watching with a lazy grin.

"We are tight," I answer. "We're like family."

"That's nice."

"Yeah." I exhale slowly. "Well, we have to be."

Her brow creases. "Why?"

"I don't know." I think about it for a moment. "Maybe because we're all we've got."

JENNA: Did you see the email from Preston?

HOLLIE: About the memorial in the hall today?

JENNA: Yeah.

HOLLIE: I saw it. What, you think I should go?

JENNA: Maybe. If you feel ready.

HOLLIE: You don't think I'd get totally hated on? This is Colleen's day.

JENNA: You don't have to hide away like this, like you're guilty.

HOLLIE: Thank you for sticking by me.

JENNA: Always.

JENNA

I arrive at Preston a little after midday. Kate's house is a couple of blocks from school, and it only takes me about five minutes to walk there. Sometimes, it feels as though I'm the only person in Gardiners Bay who travels anywhere on foot. After I turned sixteen last year, Kate started offering me her car and occasionally suggesting I save up for one myself. Everyone at Preston drives, which is evident from the habitually packed campus parking lot.

Today, there are even more cars than usual. All the spaces have been taken, and a couple of cars are even parked on the grassy quad. The lot is teeming with groups of people dressed in black, arms linked as they walk solemnly toward the building.

I check my phone before I follow the crowd into the school.

Hollie's last message is still highlighted on my screen.

I can't come today. I'm sorry.

That's all she said. And I get it. Now that I'm here, I can't help but think she's right to avoid this. She may have deleted her social media accounts, but the comments and threads about her still show up. I still see them. Fair or not, Hollie's in the firing line. She's still a suspect in Colleen's murder case. Some of the Preston girls are even spinning the narrative that Colleen was a victim of Hollie's merciless bullying and took her own life because of it.

I trail behind a group of junior girls as the flow of bodies moves into the Main Hall. The rows of long oak pews are already nearly full, and at the front of the room there's a memorial for Colleen, where people have placed candles and flowers around her last school picture.

I slide into an empty space at the back as our school principal, Mrs. Gordon, steps up to the podium at the front.

She smiles sadly at the mourners.

"Welcome," she says, and the voices simmer. "I want to thank you all for being here today. I'm sure seeing so many of you come together like this would have made Colleen very happy." She wipes a tear from the corner of her eye.

I look around the room, picking out the faces I know.

Serena is in a pew on the opposite side of the hall with Imogen, Brianna, and some of the other girls from the cheerleading squad. I catch Serena's gaze, and she presses her lips together. She tucks a strand of her sleek black hair behind her ear and looks down at her hands.

I turn back to Mrs. Gordon as she begins her speech in gentle, soothing tones. Her words are touching, actually. It makes me wonder if she knew Colleen personally or if her sentiment is simply a tribute to the tragedy of the situation, rather than the person. Colleen wasn't the girl on the honor roll whose schedule was jammed with extra-curriculars. She was the girl smoking in the upper-class bathroom and flipping off teachers. She was the girl who got kicked off the cheerleading squad after a dozen disciplinaries. But the words of love and comfort Mrs. Gordon uses reflect none of this. It's all about the tragedy, the loss, the misfortune.

Miss Keeley, the cheerleading coach, is next to take the podium. She talks about what a bright and enthusiastic girl Colleen was, and then segues on to the dangers of underaged drinking and walking home alone at night. The parents seated in the audience mutter between themselves, already formulating plans on how to get their daughters to abstain from drinking. A group of moms in the row behind me are brainstorming a fund-raiser to fit safety barriers along the coastal paths. They're all strategizing on how they can stop another tragedy.

My stomach turns. Everyone's treating this like it's just some terrible accident. They're carefully painting Colleen as a poor girl who, after too much alcohol, slipped and fell from the coastal cliff path into the water. The girl they're mourning today is not Colleen—it's the image of the girl they wish she'd been. I guess it's more palatable that way.

It's as though the people here have closed their eyes to the fact that someone in their peaceful, wholesome town could be capable of the most brutal crime.

Murder.

Some members of the cheer squad come to the podium to read a poem. Imogen and Brianna are among the girls, but Serena stays seated.

Serena is the captain of the squad, yet she's not standing with the team to read the poem?

My gaze lingers on her. She slips out her phone and starts tapping on the keypad. She's texting. She's actually texting while the rest of her squad reads out their poignant verses.

I turn back to the front of the hall when Mrs. Gordon returns to conclude the ceremony.

As people begin to leave, I squeeze through the crowd following after Serena.

"Hey," I call, catching up with her on the quad. "Serena, wait."

She turns in surprise. "Oh. Hey, Jenna." Her dark eyes look a little red, like she's been crying.

"Are you okay?"

She glances around and her raven hair flutters in the breeze. "Yeah. I'm fine. I mean, I'm sad. But I'm…y'know." She pauses. "Shit. Are *you* okay? This must bring up some bad memories. I mean, of finding Colleen and all."

"Bring up memories? They haven't gone away yet."

She presses her hand to her mouth. Her scarlet nail polish glistens in the slanted afternoon light. "I'm so sorry you had to go through that." Another pause. "Listen, I'm sorry I haven't been there for you through this. I'm a shitty friend."

"It's fine," I say, catching some of my own flyaway strands. "You've been busy with cheerleading, and Max…"

She waves her hand. "No. That's no excuse. I should have reached out to you more. You know, after."

"Honestly, Serena, it's fine."

"We're still good, aren't we?" She reaches out and touches my arm. There's something vulnerable in her expression.

Something that makes me feel kind of sorry for her. Hollie and I have spent these past few months thinking she's a total social climber for replacing us with Imogen and Brianna and the cheer girls, and maybe she is. But, she's still Serena. She's still the girl who I've poured my heart out to over many a tub of cookie dough ice cream.

"We're good," I assure her.

She glances back at the school as swarms of mourners dressed in black descend. "This is a lot, right?"

My eyes linger on a group of people hugging and crying around the picnic tables. "Yeah. Tell me about it."

"I've got to get out of here," Serena mutters. "I can't deal with this right now."

"I get it. I'll call you sometime." It's been a while since I called Serena. It's been a while since she called me, for that matter.

"You wanna come with me? I could use some company. I'm guessing you could, too?"

"Okay," I say slowly. "Where do you want to go?"

She jingles her car keys, and a little diamante shoe pendant swings from the key ring. "I don't know. Anywhere that isn't here."

I take one last look at the school and the clusters of teary-eyed people heading our way. "I'm in."

She grabs my arm, and we pace toward her car. I remember her parents surprising her with this car for her sweet sixteen—a sleek black Porsche with a personalized license plate, SERENITY1. She climbs into the driver's side, and I slide into the low passenger seat. A strawberry-scented air freshener hovers between us. In fact, the whole car smells like sweet strawberries and cigarettes. Serena starts the engine, and we pull out of the parking lot just as queues are beginning to form.

Suddenly, being alone with her makes me aware of the distance the past few months has brought between us. It's as if I don't know what to say to her anymore. All the things we used to talk about, like last night's episode of whatever show we're binging or who said what at lunch, just don't seem important any more. I don't know what she's binge watching. I don't know what's going on in her life, period.

I wait a moment before I ask, "Were you texting?"

She throws me a quick glance. "Huh?"

"During the service. You were on your phone."

"Oh. Yeah."

"Who were you texting?"

"Just Max. Something in that poem made me think of him."

"Oh. Okay."

She reaches down to the cup holder and checks her cell. "He hasn't responded yet. But he will. Sometimes it takes him a while to check his messages."

We fall silent.

"How are things going with Max?" I ask as we cruise along the suburban street.

"Good. Really good. Can you believe it's been six months?" She glances at me again as she drives, probably waiting for me to show my amazement.

"Wow." I muster a smile. "It's pretty serious, huh?"

"Mm-hmm."

"That's great. I'm happy for you."

She taps her scarlet fingernails on the steering wheel. "I mean, I know we had that fight a little while back, but we're over that now." Her nose twitches.

Of course I know the fight she's referring to. Max showed up at Preston right before summer break, and they had a heated argument in the middle of the parking lot. That night, Serena deleted all his photos from her social media pages and announced that she was "done."

Although Hollie and I watched the fight from the sidelines, we couldn't pinpoint *exactly* what it was about. And Serena certainly wasn't telling. As near as I could figure, it seemed like Max had been flirting with other girls and Serena had busted him. She was crying, screaming, the works. I thought then that Max seemed like a jerk. He smirked and charmed his way out of it—eventually. It's no wonder Serena forgave him, he has the whole rebel-without-a-cause thing down to a fine art.

They were back together by the following week, and their lovey-dovey pictures gradually started to reappear.

"So, things are good now?" I ask.

"Better than good. I'm in love." She hesitates and chews her thumbnail. "Sure, he has his moments, but who doesn't, right?"

I frown. "He has his moments? What does that mean?"

"Nothing. Just, Max is kind of complicated."

"Complicated, how?"

"I don't know. His past was pretty messed up, and I think that makes him act a little volatile sometimes, y'know?" Her eyes dart to me. "Don't go broadcasting this, but he had a seriously effed-up childhood. Like, his dad's in prison and stuff."

"Oh." I don't know why I'm taken aback by this. It's no secret that the Rooks all have a past. Hence why they've ended up at Rookwood. They're not pampered and privileged like the Preston girls.

"So, sometimes," Serena carries on, "Max screws up. Sometimes. But doesn't everyone?"

I'm glad her attention is on the approaching stoplight because otherwise she'll see the dubious expression that I know is on my face. Sure, I feel bad for Max if his life has been tough, but that doesn't give him a free pass to treat his girlfriend like crap. To treat anyone like crap.

"Hey," she says as we roll to a stop at the red light. "I know what we can do today. We should totally go to Rookwood!"

I can't even pretend to share her enthusiasm. I check the clock on the dash. "But it's the middle of the afternoon on a Monday. Won't they have classes?"

She gives an easy wave of her hand. "They'll be finished by now. Trust me, it'll be fun. The weekdays there aren't wild like the weekend parties are. You'll like it."

I crinkle my nose.

"And," she adds, "I really want you to get to know Max. It's been six months, and you've hardly spent any time with him."

"I've been to a few parties," I remind her.

"Exactly. You're one of my best friends, Jenna, and you don't know anything about my boyfriend."

"I know his dad's in jail," I say, offering a smile.

"Shh," she hisses, flapping her hands.

I laugh. "What, you think he's bugged your car?"

"No." She swats at me as the red light changes to green. "Just forget I said that, though, okay?"

I mime zipping my lips shut. "I'm one of your best friends, huh? I thought Brianna and Imogen had taken that spot."

She grins. "Brianna and Imogen are cool, but you're my ride or die."

I laugh again.

"I'm glad we're hanging out, just us. It's been forever since we've done this."

I twist in my seat, turning to face her. "Yeah. Why, exactly? You totally ditched Hollie and me over the summer."

Her lips purse. "I didn't mean to, Jenna. Things just got…" She trails off and sighs. "I don't know. I'm sorry. I've really missed you."

"I've missed you, too."

We take off along the coastal road, where the boutique shops and artisan cafes line the walkway. Palm leaves sway gently in the breeze, and beyond the promenade, the ocean catches the light and glistens.

Serena veers left onto the side streets. Evidently, the decision has been made. We're going to Rookwood.

Great.

Although, maybe this isn't such a terrible idea. If I'm going to go, it may as well be in broad daylight. And if there's any chance of snooping for information that could clear Hollie's name, this could be my way in.

It only takes a couple of minutes to reach the Rookwood entrance sign, with its gold calligraphy on a rusted black panel. But Serena bypasses the courtyard entrance. I catch a glimpse of the gothic school building as we pass it by. It somehow manages to look grim even on a reasonably bright day.

We carry on along a track through the forest and eventually roll to a stop in a glade. I can just about see the cabin's roof through the firs.

Leaving the comfort of Serena's car, we forge a path through the trees toward the cabin. In the daylight, it takes on a new face, and I can imagine it was probably quite pretty once. Inside, it's as dark as if it were nighttime, blushed by low watt bulbs and hazy with smoke. I follow Serena as she greets a couple of guys lounging on the couches. Max is across the room, shooting pool with another boy. Serena skips over to him, dragging me with her.

"Baby!" She jumps into Max's arms and wraps her legs around his waist.

After what feels like an eternity, they break apart, and she bounces back down to the floor.

"This is Jenna," Serena introduces me. "She's been my bestie for, like, forever."

"Hey." Max is blond-haired and blue-eyed, and in a parallel universe he would have slotted right into the role of captain of the football team or prom king. But in this universe, there's a coldness to him, and something calculating in his eyes despite his charming smile. Something that makes me bristle.

"This is Max," Serena says, as if I don't already know. "And Tommy."

The boy holding the pool cue looks up.

"Hi." I try to keep my smile easy. Tommy. The boy from the picture. The one with jet-black hair and bottomless eyes. The third name.

"Hey," he says.

Max returns his attention to Serena. "What brings you here, babe?"

"I just missed you, baby. I wanted to see you." She nuzzles into his chest, and he strokes her back. There's a pause, then she asks, "Why didn't you reply to my text?"

His brow furrows. "What text?"

"I sent it about an hour ago."

"I didn't see a text."

She exhales. "Oh, good. I thought that was it. I just wanted to check."

I'm starting to wonder if Serena's teary eyes after the service had less to do with Colleen and everything to do with Max and his radio silence. That would explain why she was so insistent on showing up here.

I can't stop my gaze from wandering across the room, toward the couches. Colleen's last Instagram picture was taken just a few feet from where I'm standing.

"Hello."

I jump at the sound of Adam's voice.

"You're here," he says. He's smiling. It's a kind of cute, lopsided grin that I haven't seen on him before.

Serena untangles herself from Max. "Oh, hey, Adam. This is my friend Jenna."

"I know," he says.

Serena frowns, and then her face drops into a look of understanding. "Oh, right. Because you two…" She trails off, biting her lower lip.

Max looks between us. "You two, what?"

I see the tension in Adam's jaw. "Nothing."

But Serena is already diving into the explanation. "Jenna was there, too," she says, delicately. "When Adam found Colleen."

Serena seems oblivious to the sudden uneasiness amongst the three boys. Their eyes move between each other, Max to Adam, Adam to Tommy, Tommy to Max.

"Is that right?" Max says at last. "I had no idea." His piercing blue gaze is back on me now. "That must have been upsetting for you."

I don't flinch under his stare. "It was," I say, calmly. There's a hidden meaning in his words, in his inflection. I'm just not sure what the undertone means. It feels like a warning, or a threat.

"I've seen her story all over the news," he adds. "Some wasted girl slips and falls from the cliff edge, right? Sad."

I fold my arms. "Yes, it is sad. Colleen came here a lot, didn't she? She came to your parties."

Tommy shrinks back.

Serena puts her hands on her hips and stares at Max's profile. "You didn't hang out with her, though, did you? I know she was always coming over here, but you didn't hang out with her one-on-one. Right?"

Max's eyebrows draw together. "No. Of course not."

"Colleen used to come here sometimes," Serena tells me. "But the guys weren't friends with her." She turns to Max again. "Were you?"

"No. I don't even remember the girl." He raises an eyebrow, as though he's daring anyone to challenge him. As though he's daring *me* to challenge him.

Adam rests his hand on my arm. "Do you want the tour? I can show you around while these guys finish their game." He glances at Tommy, and on command Tommy lifts his pool cue.

"Your shot," Tommy tells Max.

Max steps away from Serena and lifts his own cue. Suddenly, I notice the tattoo on his forearm—it's the same inked talon that Adam has on his arm. And Tommy has one, too. "See you around," Max says to me as he chalks the blue tip. "Jenna, isn't it?"

"Yes," I answer, as coolly as I can.

"I'll remember that," he says.

Adam guides me to the door, and it creaks as he opens it. We cross outside onto the mossy ground. The smell of pine engulfs the salty air.

We're alone now.

I wrap my arms around myself as the wind whistles through the trees. "What was that about?"

"What?"

"You know what." I hold his stare. "Max. What's his deal?"

Adam presses his lips together. "Look, it's nothing. Max just doesn't trust people easily, that's all. If you come around here asking about Colleen, it's going to put him on edge. We've already had the cops asking questions just 'cause she partied with us sometimes."

My eyes travel over the cabin and the ivy crawling up the log walls. "I don't buy that. I've been questioned too, but I'm not acting sketchy. Something's up."

"Nothing's up." He lowers his voice to a murmur. "We knew Colleen, yeah. But none of us have anything to do with what happened to her. None of us *want* to have anything to do with that. We don't want our names involved."

"My friend," I say, "the girl that I told you about, Hollie, she doesn't *want* to have anything to do with this, either."

"I know." He runs his hand across his brow. "And I'm sorry about that."

"But if you or your friends know anything that could—"

"I don't. I'm sorry."

"Are you covering for Max?"

He shakes his head. "No. There's nothing to cover. I'm just looking out for him, like how you're looking out for Hollie. I don't want him getting dragged into this."

"But if you're hiding something..."

"Jenna—" my name sounds careful on his lips "—you have to drop this. Stop asking about Colleen. Stop asking about Max."

"Why? If he's got nothing to hide—"

"Stop." He glances over his shoulder, checking that we're alone. "We look out for each other here."

Around us, the trees move, their branches bowing in the wind.

I keep my gaze on Adam. "What does that mean?"

"Max isn't hiding anything. And you have to stop asking me about this."

"Oh." I breathe out a laugh. "I get it. Max isn't hiding anything. But if he were, you wouldn't tell me, right?"

He kicks the ground with the toe of his sneaker, disturbing the moss. "We look out for each other here," he echoes.

And that's all he says.

JENNA: Hey. Are you okay?

HOLLIE: I guess. How was the memorial?

JENNA: Kind of heavy. I ended up going to Rookwood with Serena right after. I'm still there.

HOLLIE: ???

JENNA: In my defense, I was in her car. I had no choice.

HOLLIE: Why were you in Serena's car?

JENNA: Long story.

HOLLIE: Do you want me to come rescue you?

JENNA: It's okay. Serena said we'll be leaving soon. Hol, I have to ask you something.

HOLLIE: Go on.

JENNA: Those times that you went to Rookwood with Serena, did you see much of Max?

HOLLIE: Obviously. Serena got drunk and introduced me to him, like, ten times in one night.

JENNA: Did you think he was shady?

HOLLIE: Totally. Why?

JENNA: Okay, I'm just going to put it out there. I think Max had something to do with what happened to Colleen.

HOLLIE: Call me when you can.

ADAM

"What was she talking to you about out there?"

"Nothing."

"She was asking about Colleen?"

"Yeah."

His grip tightens around the pool cue. "Just remember whose side you're on, Adam."

I meet his stare. "You don't do yourself any favors, Max. You were acting weird as hell."

A couple of the guys pass the pool table, and we stop talking.

"Later," Max says.

"Yeah."

I knew about Rookwood long before I was sent here. It's the place parents always threaten to send their kids whenever they act out. This dark dungeon in the middle of a forest, where all the bad kids go to rot.

Back then, I never thought I'd be one of the bad kids.

Freshmen are always fair game in the first few months. Fourteen years old, just starting out at Rookwood, and we know to keep our heads down. I leave the school building and cross through the courtyard. Tommy is farther ahead, walking toward the dorms. We've lived here a while, a couple of weeks, but he still doesn't talk much. I don't mind that. I don't feel much like talking either.

I watch him walk. His head is bowed. It always is.

A group of senior guys have gathered behind him. They're like lions stalking prey. They've formed a pack, and their strides quicken as they close in on Tommy. They have a purpose, a game. And I think, Ah well, here we go.

Tommy's head stays low, matted black hair hanging over his eyes. I think he knows what's coming. He's bracing himself.

They jump him. They get him down to the concrete and start taking pops at him. Just for fun. Just because they can.

I drop my backpack and race across the courtyard. I grab the nearest guy and pull him down. Some of the others start taking shots at me.

Through the blur of arms and fists, I see another freshman. A blond boy, swearing at the top of his lungs as he runs over. This stocky little kid starts scrapping, throwing punches at the older guys.

A whistle alarm blows, and we all scatter like crows. Like Rooks.

We didn't win the fight. Tommy and the blond kid look bloodied up. I figure I look the same.

Security come with their whistles and radios, and we run for the forest. It's better not to get caught fighting, even if it isn't your fault. No one wants to get put into isolation—that block screws with your head.

I'll never forget the rough feel of the tree trunk on my spine as I lean against it, breathless and bruised.

The blond boy starts laughing. Blood is trickling down his face, staining his teeth, but he just laughs.

It makes me smile. Tommy, too. I don't know why. I guess we're fucked up, and not just on the outside.

"What's your name?" I ask the blond boy.

"Max."

I slap my hand to his and grip hard. Then Tommy does the same.

"I think the three of us would have had them," Max says. "If we'd just had some more time."

Tommy wipes a smear of blood from his nose. "Yeah."

"Yeah," I echo. "I think we did alright. Thanks for helping out."

Max slaps my hand again. "I got you," he says.

This is our initiation. If this was a test, we all just passed. We don't have to say any more. We're going to have each other's backs now, no matter what.

JENNA

We pull up outside my house, and Serena cuts the engine. Dusk is starting to set, and the lampposts have come on. Kate's car isn't in the driveway, which means she's probably still at the precinct.

"So?" Serena turns in her seat. She's beaming at me.

I blink back at her.

"Max?" she prompts. "He's great, right?"

I can't seem to manage a response.

"He's the best." She answers her own question with a satisfied smile.

"Yeah. He was acting pretty weird when I asked him about Colleen, though."

"Probably because she's dead. Everyone acts weird when you talk about dead people, Jenna. It's a thing."

"But he made out like he didn't even know her."

"Because he didn't. Not really."

"She used to party at that cabin every weekend."

"Not every weekend," Serena says with a frown. "Colleen

tagged along sometimes, but the guys never actually hung out with her."

"That's not how Colleen saw it."

Her eyes cloud. "What do you mean? How did Colleen see it?"

"She thought the Rooks were her friends. She made out like she and Max were really tight."

Serena's mouth pulls into a grimace. "Max barely even knew who she was. Colleen was effing delusional."

A coldness comes over me. I don't like talking about Colleen this way. Okay, Colleen and I were hardly best friends, but still, it feels disrespectful.

"I'd better go," I tell Serena. "Kate will be home soon, and it's my turn to cook dinner."

She blows air kisses at me. "Bye, J. See you at school tomorrow."

"Yeah. See you."

I step out from the bathroom stall. There's a girl standing in front of the mirror. She glances my way.

"Oh," I say. "Hey, Colleen."

She turns back to the mirror and resumes sweeping her mascara brush over her lashes. "You got any gum?" she asks.

"Sorry, no." I move to one of the sinks and turn on the faucet.

She frowns at me. "Perfume? Anything?"

"Nope."

She struts across the bathroom and leans in close to me. "Smell me. Can you tell I've smoked a joint?"

"Um…"

She rolls her eyes. "Come on, Jenna. Do I smell of pot? Yes or no." She snaps her fingers, hurrying me along.

"Kind of," I tell her.

"Shit." She twists her platinum hair to one side and dips down to the running faucet. She swills out her mouth, then splashes water over her face.

I watch her.

"Okay." She pops back up and leans close to me again. "That's better, right?"

"I don't know. Maybe a little. But you still smell like pot."

Her shoulders sink. "Ah, well. Screw it, right? It's not like my mom's going to get that close."

"Haven't you been in classes all day? When did you find time to smoke pot?"

She turns to the mirror and pouts at her reflection. "I bailed on fourth and fifth. I've been at Rookwood."

My eyebrows rise, and she laughs.

"Jesus, Jenna. Looks like you could use a joint yourself. Loosen up a little, babe." She tugs at a strand of my hair, then laughs again.

I smooth the hair back down. "Personal space, Colleen."

"Why don't you ever come to Rookwood? I thought you and Serena were solid?"

"Not anymore, apparently. She has Imogen and Brianna now."

A cackle escapes her cerise lips. "Yeah, because they're fun. They know how to have a good time."

"At Rookwood." My tone is dry. "Awesome."

"Whatever. Serena doesn't need you. She has her fake friends to party with now."

"Imogen and Brianna aren't fake friends."

Colleen snorts. "You don't know the half."

"Well, good for you guys. Rookwood parties are not for me."

"Oh, what?" she scoffs. "Because it's not a library or wherever it is that you basics like to go?"

I cross my arms. "The Rooks are shady. I always see them hanging out at the pier, graffitiing or getting wasted."

"So? If you weren't so judgmental, you might actually find that you like some of them. Those guys are basically my new best friends." She gazes at her reflection and combs her fingers through her silky hair. *"Max is cool."*

"Max? As in, Serena's boyfriend, Max?"

"Yeah."

I crinkle my nose. "Max is your new best friend?"

"Yeah."

"How does Serena feel about that?"

"Jealous AF. Obviously."

ADAM

We meet in the forest at midnight. Max, Tommy, and me. There's a clearing about half a mile in where we've set up logs around a firepit. We come here sometimes. Usually, when we want to be alone.

I hold up my phone's flashlight as Max throws some kindling onto the pit. He strikes a match, and a flame glows orange around his thumb and forefinger. I watch as he tosses the lit matchstick onto the tinder and the embers start to burn.

Tommy sits on one of the logs. Max stays standing. I do, too.

"So, this girl Jenna," Max says. "She's asking about Colleen?"

I shrug.

"What, were they friends or something?"

"I don't know," I answer. "Maybe."

Tommy drops his head into his hands.

"And what are you telling her?" Max is eye-level with me.

Neither of us moves. "What are you saying when she's asking questions?"

"What'd you think? Nothing."

His jaw clenches. "It'd better be nothing, Adam."

I don't bother responding. I take a seat next to Tommy and start prodding the smoldering kindling with a twig, trying to get the flames to rise.

Max is pacing and muttering to himself.

"We're screwed," Tommy says under his breath. "We've already got the cops looking into us. The last thing we need is some girl finding out about anything."

I stare into the growing fire as it crackles and hisses. "She won't."

Tommy catches my gaze. The firelight illuminates his face in patches, leaving his eyes as two dark shadows. "I can't get kicked out of school, Adam. I'm still on probation. I'll get locked up for this."

"It won't come to that."

Max stops pacing and takes a seat on the log opposite us. His knee starts bouncing.

"She can't come around here anymore." He's nervous. I can hear the fear building in his voice as he speaks into the fire. "This Jenna. You can't bring her around here." His eyes land on me.

I frown back at him. "I didn't bring her. Serena brought her, not me."

"We agreed, remember?" Max's pale gaze darts over both of us now. "We've got a plan. We've just gotta stick to it. Yeah?"

Neither of us replies. We don't have to.

Max's stare settles on Tommy. "Get your shit together, T."

Tommy mumbles a response. His head is bowed, fingers knotted through his dark hair.

I snap the twig and toss the pieces into the flames. "He's fine," I tell Max. "Me and him are all good. You're the one who needs to get his shit together."

Max stays focused on the fire. He has nothing left to say.

I try not to watch, but I can't bring myself to look away. They're on the sofa. Colleen's talking fast, and Max is consoling her, stroking her arm and whispering into her ear. Every now and then, he glances across the room, checking that we're still alone.

Checking that Serena isn't here to see this.

He's cool with Tommy and me shooting pool at the back of the cabin, but if anyone else were to show up now, this wouldn't look good.

Man, Serena would flip.

Suddenly, Colleen's voice starts getting louder. She stands up, blond hair flying.

"Calm down," Max tells her. "Relax, Colleen. Please."

"To hell with you." She yanks her arm away from his touch. "Don't tell me to calm down. You calm down, asshole! You think you can manipulate me that easily?"

He glances across the room at Tommy and me. We pretend to care about our pool game, swapping quick looks over the table.

"Should we step in?" Tommy mouths.

I shake my head.

But Colleen's really losing it. She's screaming, cussing, the works.

"I'm sorry," Max says. He's standing now, too. "I messed up. It was a mistake—"

She chokes out an angry sound. "Oh, a mistake?"

"I'm with Serena. I love Serena."

She erupts into bitter laughter. "You're full of it!"

Tommy props his pool cue against the table.

I wince. "Tommy, don't get involved."

It's too late. He's already crossing the room, heading toward them. "Colleen," Tommy's saying in that practiced calm voice that the Rookwood teachers use on us sometimes. "Slow down. Just breathe."

She glares at him.

"Do you want to go somewhere and talk?" Tommy asks. "Just me and you?"

"In case you haven't noticed, I'm having a conversation with Max."

Max looks down at the floor.

"I don't think that's a good idea right now," Tommy says. "This is getting too heated. You need to back off."

"Are you kidding me?" she banshee-screams at him.

"Colleen," Tommy carries on. "I'm only trying to help. I care about you. We all do."

"Yeah, right! You don't give a shit about me. You assholes don't give a shit about anyone but each other. You Rooks are all the same!"

Colleen lashes out at Max then, slapping his face in a round of quick cracks. He pushes her away, and she stumbles backward.

Suddenly, I'm involved too.

Tommy and I are in between them, trying to hold her back. I tense as she claws at my arm, trying to get to Max. My heart is racing.

"You're done," she screams. "All of you." Her wild eyes dart to Max. "I'm going to tell Serena exactly what you've been doing behind her back!"

Max's jaw clenches.

"And you—" she points at Tommy with a trembling hand "—don't test me. Remember I know your secret."

His secret?

I stop. Tommy and Max do, too. It's as though her words have frozen all three of us, turning the air to ice with one sharp shot.

"All of you," she says. "Your shitty lives may as well be over. You're nobodies," she spits. "You're all nobodies on a fast track to juvie." She looks at me. "Oh, and don't think I've forgotten about you, Adam. I heard about your poor mom, by the way. You really are cold-blooded, aren't you? Ruthless. I'll make sure I spread the word about that." She blows me a kiss.

Clean sweep. She has us all.

JENNA

I shouldn't be doing this. I know I shouldn't be doing this.

My eyes move quickly over the document headings as I leaf through the stacks of papers. There are a ton of reports, mostly filled with police jargon that means nothing to me. I'm not looking for jargon. I'm looking for statements, names, anything that alludes to suspects.

These are the original documents, which means, knowing Kate, in a couple of days this data will be inputted into some encrypted system and the hard copies will be locked away in a dusty filing cabinet while the case resumes.

This is my only shot.

I pause on a page, and my heart skips a beat. It's a photo, an extreme close-up showing the marks around Colleen's throat. The swollen skin. The defined bruises. The finger marks.

I glance over my shoulder into the corridor. The shower is still running upstairs, and the water heater is humming from the system in the kitchen.

I take a steadying breath and keep going.

Further into the pile, there's a stack of pages held together with a paper clip. On the front cover sheet, a list of names is printed in alphabetical order.

This is it. I know it is. *Hollie Braithwaite* is near the top, among the dozens of other names on the list. Hollie's statement is in here, probably along with any other information the investigators might have gathered on her. Hers is the only name with an asterisk alongside it.

I trail my finger down the list. My own name is on here too, probably correlating to the statement I gave right after Colleen was found. There are other names I recognize, boys from Rookwood, girls from school, teachers, Colleen's family members.

Max Grayson.

I flip through the document until I find his transcript.

My eyes move fast over the text.

Interview with Max Grayson,
conducted by Detective Kate Dallas at 11:15 a.m.
on Monday, October 1st.

K.D.: What can you tell me about Colleen O'Dell?

M.G.: Not much. She knew my girlfriend.

K.D.: Your girlfriend's name, please?

M.G.: Serena. Serena Blake.

K.D.: Right. They were friends, Serena and Colleen?

M.G.: Yeah.

K.D.: We have witnesses who say you spent quite a bit of time with Miss O'Dell.

M.G.: I saw her around, yeah. Like I told you, she was friends with my girlfriend.

K.D.: Any reason why you think someone would want to hurt O'Dell?

M.G.: Beats me.

K.D.: What about you? Did you have a reason to hurt O'Dell?

M.G.: I didn't know her.

K.D.: But you spent a lot of time with her. You must have known her a little.

M.G.: Who says I spent a lot of time with her?

K.D.: I think you knew her much better than you're letting on, Max.

K.D.: Nothing to say?

M.G.: Nope.

K.D.: I'll ask you again, Max. Did you, or anyone you know, have reason to harm Miss O'Dell?

M.G.: No. Why are you even questioning me? Who told you I had anything to do with this girl?

K.D.: Does it matter?

M.G.: Yeah, it matters. Because it's a lie.

K.D.: If I've been misinformed, why don't you tell me who I should be questioning? If not you, then who?

M.G.: Maybe you should ask her friends.

K.D.: What do you mean by that, Max?

M.G.: (inaudible.)

K.D.: Speak up, please.

M.G.: Nothing. Just, they were the ones who knew her. Not me.

K.D.: Her friends? You mean like your girlfriend, Serena?

K.D.: No response?

M.G.: I don't know why you're asking me about Colleen O'Dell. I told you already, I didn't know the girl.

Upstairs, the shower stops running.

I grab my phone and take a photo of Max's transcript. Then I flip through and take photos of as many documents as I can before I gather the pages back together and return the entire pile to the folder marked *Confidential.*

My heart's pounding as I move to the kitchen and pour myself a cup of coffee. I slide into a seat at the island and flip open a lifestyle magazine that's been left out on the counter. Probably one of Kate's. I can barely focus on the article.

Kate's footsteps pad downstairs. A few seconds later, she emerges, wearing sweats and a tee, and towel drying her hair.

"Hi, Jenna," she says when she sees me seated at the island.

I flip the magazine shut. "Morning."

"You're up early."

"Am I?"

She gives me a quizzical look.

I clear my throat. "Do you want some coffee? I just made a fresh pot."

"That sounds great." She drops her damp towel onto the island while I hop up to pour her a cup.

"Late night?" I ask as the pot whirs.

She presses her lips together. "Unfortunately, yes."

"Were you working on Colleen's case?"

"Yeah. Time just got away from me."

I hand her the coffee, which she gratefully accepts.

She takes a sip, and her eyelids flutter closed for a second.

I sink back into my seat and wait for her attention to return to me. "You know Colleen was friends with some of the Rookwood boys," I begin. "Have you talked to the students there?"

"We have. But there's nothing substantial." She stares at me over the rim of her cup. "Why do you ask?"

"I don't know. Just that some of the guys at Rookwood seem a little off."

Her brow furrows. "I didn't know you'd been spending time with those boys."

It may not have been a direct question, but it was a loaded comment all the same.

I sit up a little straighter under the scrutiny of her gaze. "I haven't. Not really. But Serena's dating one of the guys who goes to the school, so…"

She nods in understanding. "Of course. Well, try not to get too involved, okay?"

"Trust me, I have no intention of it."

I think of Adam, and a knot forms in my stomach.

"I'm sure the students there are harmless, for the most part,"

Kate adds, "but I don't like the thought of what might be going on at that place. We've had way too many calls at the precinct about fights breaking out or fires started on campus." She shakes her head. "It's not something I want you getting caught up in."

"Yeah. I get it." I chew my lip.

Kate reaches across the island and squeezes my hand. "I can see how much this is affecting you. Colleen wasn't just some stranger way across the country. She was in your neighborhood. Your school. This is too close to home to ignore."

"She was murdered." My voice comes out as a whisper. "Someone killed her."

"Yes."

"Do you have leads?"

Wearily, she runs her fingers through her damp hair. "There are a few."

"And Hollie is still among them?"

Kate exhales slowly. "Yes," she admits.

"But she's not your only suspect? It could have been someone from Rookwood?"

"Jenna—"

"Kate, please." I try again. "It could have been one of the Rookwood boys, couldn't it?"

Her eyes move away from me.

That's all I'm going to get.

ADAM

"Do you think he did it?" Tommy's voice seems to echo in the darkness of our room.

I stare up at the ceiling, following the pattern of shadows with my eyes. "No," I answer at last. "Do you?"

"I don't know anymore, man. He's been acting so weird."

"We're all acting weird. Because we know how this will look for us if it gets out."

"It's already out," Tommy mutters.

"No, it isn't."

"Then why are the cops questioning us?"

"Because I found her."

His bed frame creaks as he sits up. "But Max and I didn't find her. Why are they questioning us more than you? They know something, I swear."

"Max thinks the Preston girls dropped your names because you guys used to hang out with Colleen sometimes." A hazy memory of Tommy and Colleen whispering in dark corners flashes through my mind, just like it has countless times since she showed up dead.

His secret. She knew his secret.

The bed creaks again as he drops back onto the mattress. "I'm screwed."

"Relax. You're fine. The cops questioned you, and then they realized you had nothing to do with this." I say the words. Believing them. Believing that the detectives aren't interested in him. Believing that he had nothing to do with this.

"But Max..." Tommy trails off.

"I don't think he did it."

There's a pause between us, and the wind groans outside. The pecan branches tap at our windowpane. Slow, steady raps.

Then Tommy speaks again. "Do you think *I* did it?"

"No. Do you think *I* did?"

"No," he says, quickly.

I wouldn't have blamed him if he'd have said yes. The thought had crossed my mind about him, and about Max. We were all angry that night. We all had a lot to lose, in our own ways. She threatened us, and we were scared. People react without thinking when they're scared.

When I was a kid, I tried to free a wild dog that had gotten itself caught up in some ropes. The damn dog got spooked, thought I was coming for it, and bit the hell out of my right arm while I was cutting through the rope. I learned that day that when an animal gets cornered, it bites back.

Any one of us could have bitten back that night.

After Colleen dropped her grenades and left, Max stepped outside to make a call, Tommy went back to the dorm, and I stayed at the cabin. None of us can really know for sure if anyone followed Colleen. We're going off the assumption that we trust each other. Because we always have. Because we've always had to.

"I get the feeling he knows something," Tommy says, breaking our silence. "I think he knows more than he's telling us."

I hold my focus on the ceiling as the shadows from the branches form a spider's web pattern. "Yeah. You're probably right."

The wind is howling outside. I can hear my own heartbeat in my ears.

Max is pacing around the cabin. He's raking his hands through his hair. His shirt is bunched at the front, still creased from where she grabbed him.

Tommy is staring out the window, looking into the darkness.

She's gone.

I touch my arm. The skin is red in four stripes, marks left over from where her fingernails scraped. I pull my sleeve down to cover it.

"We should go after her." Tommy's voice is hoarse.

"No," I tell him. "Don't."

Max starts for the door. "I'm going to find her."

I'm on my feet, fast. I block him. "Don't follow her. She's mad. You'll just make things worse."

The muscles in his jaw clench.

"What if she pops off again and someone hears her?" I try to reason with him. "She could blow everything up, and we'll get busted for being out here." I tug my sleeve lower, pulling the hem over my wrist. "We can't get caught bringing girls out here. Come on, man."

He shoulders past me.

"Max."

He glances back. His face is drawn. "Relax," he mutters. "I'm not going to look for her. I've got to go make a call."

He pats his pockets as he ducks outside. The wind howls, and the door slams shut behind him.

HOLLIE: Where's your head at with the Max thing?

JENNA: I don't know. I think I'm going to talk to Serena about it at school today.

HOLLIE: Bold. Are you sure about that? She won't want to hear it.

JENNA: She might know something. Maybe deep down she suspects him too?

HOLLIE: Yeah, right!

JENNA: It's worth a shot. If I can get something on Max, this could help clear your name.

HOLLIE: Well, here's hoping. Thanks, Jenna. I love you for trying.

JENNA

"Yesterday was fun."

Serena comes to a stop at my locker and hovers while I slide my books onto the lower shelf. I push the locker door shut, and she beams at me.

"Yesterday," she says again, waving her hand in front of my face like I've spaced out on her or something. "Rookwood. Me, you, ditching school after Colleen's memorial..."

"Yeah. Fun."

Her smile fades. "You didn't have fun?"

I shrug. "Rookwood."

A junior girl is loitering at her locker a couple of paces away from us. Her gaze flickers our way at the mention of Rookwood, like it's some secret world that she can only dream of.

I roll my eyes and turn back to Serena. "It's not that I didn't have fun with you, it's just..."

"What?"

"Rookwood."

"But I thought you were having a good time." She blinks

back at me. "It looked like you were getting on pretty well with Adam. You were outside talking to him for, like, ever."

"Yeah, because he was the only person I knew there. Apart from you, and you were busy."

She grins, clearly missing my point. "Oh, you *know* him, do you?"

"Well, no." I feel the heat rise to my cheeks. "I mean, I kinda know him. You know what I mean."

Serena leans against the bank of lockers and sighs. "You should have told me you weren't having fun, Jenna. We could have left sooner."

I arch an eyebrow. "Right."

"What?"

"You were a little distracted."

She frowns.

"With Max," I remind her. She really shouldn't need me to remind her of this. She was all over him from the moment we arrived, right up until the moment we left. I practically had to pry her off of him.

She smiles at me now, half-apologetic, half-smug. "He's cute, right?"

Cute is not a word I'd have used to describe Max. Kittens are cute. Max is no kitten.

I wait a couple of seconds while the junior girl abandons eavesdropping and joins the corridor foot traffic before I continue. "Now that you've mentioned it, there's actually something I wanted to talk to you about."

Serena tilts her head. "Oh, yeah? What?"

"How well do you really know Max?"

She hesitates. "He's my boyfriend. I'd say I know him pretty well." Her tone is guarded—understandably so.

"Are you sure? Are you sure you *really* know him?"

She folds her arms. "Jenna, where are you going with this?"

"Did you know that he was interviewed by the cops right after Colleen's body was found?"

"Ew, Jenna. Don't say *Colleen's body*. It's so macabre."

"Did you know that he was interviewed?"

"Yeah, apparently Colleen used to talk about him and whatever." She smooths an imaginary crease from her school sweater.

"So the police questioned Max *just* because Colleen mentioned his name around Preston?"

"Yeah. I was interviewed too," she says, flipping her glossy, black hair over her shoulder. "So were you. What's your point?"

"I was interviewed because I was there when Adam found her. You were interviewed because…"

"Because Colleen and I knew each other," she says.

"A lot of people knew Colleen," I point out. "Why did the police choose to interview Max, and then you right after?"

She swallows. There's a beat of silence before she brushes me off again. "I don't know. Because I'm captain of the cheerleading squad and Colleen used to be on the team."

She's reaching. I can hardly blame her. I'm basically insinuating that her boyfriend screwed her over. She knows it. I know it. The junior eavesdropper would have known it too if she'd stuck around long enough to hear it.

"Max sold you out to the cops." The words tumble from

my mouth, way more bluntly than I'd intended when I'd rehearsed this conversation in my head.

Her jaw drops a little. "What are you talking about?"

"Max gave your name to the police."

"Yeah, well…" She rakes her fingers through her hair. "I'm his girlfriend. They probably asked how he knew Colleen, and he probably said through me. I was the one who first brought her to the cabin parties."

I purse my lips.

Her eyes narrow. "How do you know that Max gave the cops my name, anyway? Did your aunt tell you?"

"No. I just…"

"Because I'm pretty sure that's misconduct or something."

My stomach flips. "Of course Kate didn't tell me," I backtrack. Serious damage control needed. "I'm speculating. Max must have given your name to the police, because who else would have?"

"So what if he did? Max loves me. You don't even know him, and you're acting like…" Her voice cracks, and she halts the sentence.

"Serena. Come on."

She looks away. Her eyes have started to glisten.

"Serena, I'm sorry. I'm not trying to upset you."

"Then stop talking about my boyfriend like he's this bad guy. Stop making out like you know anything about him. You don't know him."

"I'm sorry. I don't want to fight with you. I'm just trying to look out for you." I nudge her arm, and she manages a smile.

"I know you're looking out for me." She pauses and blots the corners of her eyes with the sleeve of her sweater. "But you don't have to worry about me. I'm a big girl, Jenna. I know what I'm doing."

"Okay." I'm not sure if my voice carries much conviction.

"You don't know Max," she says again.

She's right. But I can't ignore the nagging suspicion that she doesn't know Max, either. That no one really does.

I notice Imogen heading into the upper-floor bathroom at lunch, so I follow her. The door falls shut behind me.

Imogen is leaning over one of the sinks, checking her makeup in the mirror. She tucks a strand of pale-blond hair behind her ear and catches my gaze in the mirror.

"Hey."

"Hey," I reply. Imogen and I aren't friends, exactly, but we're okay. Imogen is one of the only other girls in our grade who isn't from a wealthy family. She transferred here on a scholarship, so I figure she isn't just a pretty face, she must be seriously smart too. Back in junior year, she got a B- on a test and had this huge meltdown in the science lab. It was a whole thing. I'm just banking on her being as emotionally smart as she is book smart.

She turns away from her reflection. "What's up, Jenna?"

I glance over at the bathroom stalls. The doors are all ajar. We're alone.

"Nothing," I say. "Well, something. I guess I wanted to talk to you. In private." I cringe as the words come out. There's a high chance that whatever I say to Imogen will get back to Serena. I'm not sure if that really matters at this point. Serena already knows how I feel.

"Okay," Imogen answers slowly. "Sounds heavy."

I take a deep breath. "You see a lot of Max, right?"

Her brow furrows.

"I mean, at Rookwood," I elaborate. "You go to the parties there with Serena on the weekends, don't you?"

"Yeah."

"Colleen used to go too, right?"

"Yeah." Imogen's expression is blank. Clearly, she has no idea where I'm going with this.

"So, about Max." I forge on. "What do you think of him?"

"He's okay." She combs her fingers through the ends of her hair. "I don't really know him."

"Do you get a vibe, though?"

"A vibe?" she echoes. "Like what?"

I run my hands up and down my arms. The bathroom feels cold, all of a sudden. "There's just something I don't trust about him. Serena doesn't see it. She's totally blinded by him."

"He's kind of hard to read, maybe. But they all are. The Rooks, y'know?"

"Yeah. I guess."

She leans against the sink. "Actually, Max is from my old neighborhood. His family has a pretty bad reputation."

My eyebrows rise. "I didn't realize you knew Max from before."

"Kind of my claim to fame, knowing a Rook, huh?" She gives me an ironic smile. "But honestly, I didn't really know him. We went to the same middle school, and he was always getting into trouble." She rolls her eyes. "He was that guy."

"Clearly, if he's ended up at Rookwood." I pause at the thought. "Do you know why he was sent there?"

"I think he stole a car." She holds up both hands. "But don't quote me on that. Serena probably knows more than I do."

I fall silent for a second.

"I don't think he's dangerous," Imogen adds. "If that's what you're getting at."

My gaze wanders to the mirror and lands on my own reflection. I look tense. My hands are knotted together, and my brow is creased.

"You're not so sure?" she asks.

"I'm just worried about Serena. I'm worried about what she's getting herself into with him. Can she really trust him?"

"Oh, Max is totally committed to her. I know you don't go to Rookwood parties much, but when they're together, it's like they're physically incapable of being apart for more than a few seconds. I don't think he'd do anything to jeopardize their relationship."

"Okay, but what about Colleen?" My words come out fast.

Imogen hesitates for a beat. "What about Colleen?"

"Colleen used to brag about being close with Max. Do you think Max could have had anything to do with…"

"What, her death?"

I say nothing.

"Jenna, no offense, but I think your imagination is running away with itself. Maybe because all the attention is on Hollie right now, you're looking for someone else to blame." She pulls a tube of lip gloss from her pocket and dabs on a fresh layer. "Max is only at Rookwood for stealing a car." She catches my gaze in the mirror. "Plenty of people have done way worse."

Her words hang heavily in the air.

ADAM

Classes are small at Rookwood. On a good day there are around ten of us in each. They keep the classes small deliberately— I don't think they want us to outnumber them by too much. That's probably a good idea.

There's a Code Red most days. When it happens, I try to keep my head down. I just pull on my headphones and crank up the volume while some kid loses it, flipping tables and pulling out fistfuls of his own hair.

We're in math today, and I can feel the tension building. Scotch is sitting across the room from me, near the window. He's muttering to himself. His words are sharp and fast, like he's getting frustrated. He can't figure out the calc problem and it's getting to him. He's been kicking the desk leg and rapping his knuckles on his paper for the past ten minutes.

And he just keeps on muttering under his breath.

I scan the room. Max catches my eye and smirks, like he knows what's coming. Tommy raises an eyebrow.

And then it starts. I flinch as Scotch's papers suddenly scatter across the classroom. Ms. Omar's head snaps up.

"Tyler." She calls him by his first name. Her voice is calm. All the staff here use that voice, that calm, soothing, safe-place shit. I figure they've all taken the same training course. How to Defuse a Meltdown 101. "Tyler, calm down, please."

Scotch bangs his head on the desktop. "Fuck this bullshit, man!" He throws his pen.

A couple of the guys start cheering him on—Max included.

And then Scotch is up on his feet. His desk is flipped over, and he's making a break for the exit.

I reach for my headphones. This could take a while.

Above the isolated thrash of music now eclipsing the classroom, I see Ms. Omar calling for assistance on her radio before following Scotch out of the room. He's a flight risk, for sure.

Now that she's gone and Scotch's gone, we're in bedlam. With the exception of Tommy and me, everyone's out of their seats. Half the boys have left the room, probably going to watch Scotch's hallway restraining. The other half have crowded around the lead-framed window and are looking down at the courtyard to see if Scotch manages to bust out of here.

Same shit, different day.

I can feel Tommy's eyes on me, so I slip my headphones down around my neck.

"I saw that coming like a half hour ago." He sits up higher in his seat, trying to see out into the corridor. "I can still hear him. He must be way down the hall though."

Shouting, cussing, followed by the calm-voiced reasoning.

I toss my pen down, and it rolls across my worksheet.

"Goddamn Scotch." I slump back in my seat. "I'm behind on this." I gesture to the unfinished problems on my page. "I need a full class to get this done."

Tommy arches an eyebrow. "How'd you think I feel? At least you're smart. You'll figure it out eventually."

I glance over at his worksheet. The page is mostly empty, and the answers he has given are wrong. I don't tell him.

"They should just let him leave." My attention strays across the room. The boys are still hanging out the open window, but there haven't been any cheers yet, which means Scotch is still in the building. "He wouldn't get far anyway, even if he did run."

Tyler Scotch is in Rookwood because he's got a short fuse. I like him, but man is he erratic. I've seen his parents—they come in for behavior management meetings sometimes. They seem nice, a mom and a dad, kind of docile and gentle. From what I've heard, they have other kids too, so they can't deal with Scotch's temper any more. It makes me think, if Scotch learned to bite his tongue once in a while, just chill, he could get out of Rookwood and have a home-cooked meal on the dinner table at seven o'clock every night. He could have god-damn milk and cookies before bed if he played his cards right. It doesn't work like that for Tommy, Max, and me. We don't get that option. We're in here for the long haul. No chance of parole. We all got branded "high risk."

It's a good thing none of us want to go home.

Max bursts into the classroom with a wild grin on his face. "Scotch is losing it! You guys need to go watch!" Max is practically bouncing, loving every second of this. "They're trying to get him into isolation, but he keeps getting past them!"

Tommy stares at the door again. The commotion has faded now.

Max bounds across the room and drags a chair next to me.

He lowers his voice. "Hey. Have you heard what the Preston girls are saying about Colleen?"

"What do you mean?"

"Serena says the cops are looking into some senior girl. Apparently, some shady text messages got leaked to the cops. Now everyone thinks this girl did it." There's an easiness in his pale blue eyes and a flicker of a smile.

I think of Jenna. Is this her friend, Hollie? It has to be.

"Smile, man." Max slaps my shoulder. "We're in the clear."

Yeah. At someone else's expense.

Max's chair scrapes as he stands abruptly. He pats me on the shoulder again before bounding away to join the guys at the window who are on Scotch watch.

On the other side of me, Daniel Harlow is talking to Tommy. Their heads are bowed close together, and they're muttering in hushed voices. Too quiet for me to hear. I don't think I want to know what they're talking about, anyway.

A moment later, Daniel slips a bill into Tommy's palm.

My fists ball on the desk.

When Daniel steps away, I turn to Tommy. He presses his lips together and casts his eyes downward.

I knew it. When I saw him talking to one of Serena's friends the other night, I knew what he was doing. I just didn't want to believe it.

"I thought you were done with this after everything that happened with Colleen?"

"I was." He still won't look at me. "I am. It's just a one-time thing."

I run a hand over my brow. "Why are you still doing this, Tommy?"

"I need the money," he mutters.

"So, you *are* still selling? Even after Colleen threatened to bust you?"

He casts a glance at the window. His jaw is tense.

"She said she knew your secret," I remind him under my breath. "And I doubt she's the only one. A whole load of those Preston girls probably know you're dealing."

Silence.

"They're not like us," I go on. "You can't trust them. If the cops find out, they'll be all over your ass for this."

He shakes his head. "I'm careful around the Preston girls."

"Careful didn't work with Colleen. You need to stop. Before you get caught."

"I can't." He rakes his hands through his shaggy hair. "You don't understand."

"I do," I tell him. But he doesn't believe me.

He looks to the side. "Anyway, this isn't the only secret Colleen knew."

The moment I see his dad, everything I know about Tommy makes sense.

The guy's stepping out of Principal Lomax's office after their behavior management meeting. It's routine, all the parents have to check in a couple of times a semester to get updates on their kid's progress. Tommy's folks don't show up that often, and now I understand why not.

They just don't give a damn.

His hand is on Tommy's shoulder, fingers gripping his shirt too tightly. Too roughly. He looks like Tommy, but an older version, with harsher features and a grim expression. His mouth is pursed. His eyes are dark.

I glance up from the water cooler. Tommy won't look at me.

I take my time pouring water while I try to catch the words exchanged.

The man's voice is lowered. "You got any cash?"

Tommy pats his pockets. "I... I don't know." He's mumbling, stooping. "I don't have much."

"But you got some?"

"A little."

"Can you spare any for your old man? They subsidize here, don't they?" He keeps a grip on Tommy's shoulder.

I watch out the corner of my eye as Tommy fumbles for his wallet and hands his dad a couple of bills.

The guy takes them and stuffs them into his jacket pocket before releasing his hold on Tommy's shoulder. Then he slips a baggie into Tommy's shirt pocket and walks away. Tommy hunches as he watches him leave.

GARDINERS BAY DAILY PRESS

Friday, October 12th

John and Esther O'Dell would like to invite friends and family to a vigil on the North Point Pier in remembrance of their beloved daughter, Colleen.

Commemorations will begin at 7:00 p.m. this evening.

Please contact Gardiners Bay council for information regarding donations and well wishes.

JENNA

"Hey, Jenna."

I turn, still towel drying my hair after gym class.

Serena is wearing her green-and-white cheer uniform with an embroidered *P* stitched across the chest. She fiddles with the end of her jet-black ponytail. I recognize that twitchy look on her. But it's been a while since I've seen it. She's nervous about something.

I stop dabbing at my hair and let the damp towel drop onto the bench. "Hey. What's up?" It's been a few days since I confronted her about Max, and we haven't really spoken since.

"I was just wondering how Hollie's doing?"

I exhale slowly. "Honestly, I don't know. These past couple of weeks have been really tough on her."

"Yeah. I keep thinking I'll see her in class, but she must not be ready to come back yet." Serena dips her gaze for a second. "Would you…" She pauses, takes a breath. "Could you let her know that I've been thinking of her? And that I'm not part of any of this."

My gaze flickers across the locker room to where Brianna and Imogen are examining themselves in the mirrors. They're wearing only their cheer skirts and bras as they contour their cheekbones like pros. Serena may not have been a part of the trolling, but her friends most definitely were.

"I've tried to reach out to Hols," Serena adds, drawing my attention back to her, "but she never replies to my texts anymore."

I run my hand over my brow. "She's not really opening up to me, either."

"Poor Hollie," Serena murmurs. "I wish there was something we could do."

"She'll get through this. The truth will come out soon, and then everything can go back to normal." I don't know if I'm saying this for Serena's benefit or my own. Either way, I'm not sure I believe it.

"I just want her to know that I'm thinking of her. That I'm…"

Brianna skips over to us and threads her arm through Serena's. Her auburn hair is perfectly coiffed, post-gym, and she's applied a whole new layer of makeup.

"What are you guys talking about?" The question is directed at Serena rather than me. I'm pretty sure there's a flash of fear in her eyes, as if she's afraid her beloved queen may revolt and return to her former friend group.

"I was just asking how Hollie's doing," Serena explains. "She wasn't in class again today. I'm worried about her."

Brianna attempts a sympathetic pout. "Oh. Poor Hols."

I can feel the cynicism creeping into my expression, probably evident from my raised eyebrows and pursed lips.

It's almost funny seeing Brianna now, all wide-eyed with sympathy, like she and the other cheerleaders weren't freezing Hollie out just a couple of weeks ago. Apparently, now that Serena is back on Team Hollie, her lackeys are quick to follow suit.

"Imogen and I have tried texting her too." Brianna echoes Serena's sentiment. "But we never hear anything back."

"Hollie's got a lot on her mind." Maybe my tone is a little clipped, because Serena gives me a look.

"Come on, Jenna," she says, gently, "we're sorry. We reacted, and we didn't help the situation. I get that. But even you have to admit, we had every reason to be suspicious of Hollie. We *have* every reason to be suspicious. We all saw the text messages."

I cross my arms. "Yes, the text messages that were leaked to the investigators."

Serena holds my stare. "It wasn't me, Jenna."

"Me, either," Brianna jumps in. "And it wasn't Imogen. The police must have pulled the texts from Hollie's records."

Serena shakes her head. "Guys, we shouldn't turn against each other. I'm just saying, we had reason to be suspicious of Hollie. They had that fight, and then Hollie told Colleen to…" she lowers her voice, "…kill herself."

I flinch.

"But this is an olive branch," Serena carries on. "We want to support Hollie. We want to believe her. Just…" She gives way to a flustered breath. "Just tell her I was asking about her, okay?"

I don't answer right away. "Sure."

"Have you heard Colleen's mom's having a vigil tonight?" she asks. "At the pier. You should come with us."

Brianna sucks in a breath, and her brow creases. But Serena doesn't seem to notice the adverse reaction to the invite.

Serena reaches out and takes my hand. "Please come with us."

"I don't know how my aunt would feel about me going out at night after what happened to Colleen. I don't know how *I* feel about it."

"Same. But Mrs. O'Dell has arranged security, and I think it would mean a lot to her if we all showed up."

I trail my fingers through the ends of my damp hair.

"I'm driving," she adds, before I have chance to respond. "I'll pick you up at seven."

"Hey, girls!" Imogen calls. She's tightening her blond ponytail as she approaches from across the room. Her cheer skirt swishes around her tanned legs. "Move your asses or we'll be late for practice." Her gaze slides over me. Sometimes I get the feeling that she's as wary of me as Brianna is.

Serena glances at the wall clock. "Is it three o'clock already?"

Brianna gives a high-pitched squeal. "Oh, shit. I've got to get dressed!" She adjusts her bra before dashing back across the locker room. Imogen follows her, and I see them whispering, heads dipped close together.

No prizes for guessing what—or *who*—they're whispering about. I'm standing right here.

"For the record," Serena adds, still hovering at my gym locker, "I meant it when I said that I want to support Hollie. I don't think Hollie did anything to Colleen."

"Of course she didn't, Serena. You know Hollie as well as I do."

The last of the P.E. stragglers filter out into the hallway, including Brianna and Imogen. Only Serena and I are left. Without the sound of hair dryers blasting, or showers running, or the tinny echo of conversation, suddenly there's an eerie silence in the damp room.

I'm seconds away from blurting out that I think Max seems like the shadiest person of all and it's him who should be under the microscope.

But I hold my tongue and steady my voice. "So, if not Hollie, who do you think killed Colleen?"

"Your guess is as good as mine."

"What is your guess?"

She shrugs. "No clue."

"Come on, Serena. You must have thought about it. You must have your suspicions."

"Honestly, Jenna—" Serena glances over her shoulder, checking that we're alone "—I don't know, and I'm not sure I want to know."

With that, she turns and walks away, her sleek black ponytail swishing behind her.

It's kind of weird seeing them sitting at our lunch table, but I suppose I should be used to it by now.

Imogen, Brianna, and Colleen, all flocking around Serena and occupying most of our former stomping grounds.

"Should we even go over there?" Hollie nudges me with her elbow, her lunch tray balanced in her hands. "We could sit somewhere else. There's an empty table at the back."

My gaze wanders across the cafeteria to Hollie's proposed table. Right next to the garbage cans. Fabulous.

"No. We should sit at our table. Just because the cheer girls are there doesn't mean we can't be there too."

Hollie gives me a dubious look.

"There are two free seats. And Serena is still our friend." I head across the crowded lunchroom, and Hollie trails behind me. I'm pretty sure I can hear her cussing at me under her breath.

I set my tray down on the table. The cheer girls stop their conversation and stare at me like I'm an alien invading.

There's a beat of silence as Hollie and I take our seats.

"Hi!" Serena says, brightly.

"Hi," Imogen echoes.

Colleen flips her blond ponytail over her shoulder. "Oh, you got the meatloaf." Her baby-blue eyes stray over our lunch trays. "Brave. Remind me not to sit near you in Math. That rotten meat reeks."

Brianna giggles.

And just like that, their conversation resumes.

Hollie and I exchange a look.

"So, Friday," Imogen says, her eyes fixed on Serena, "I'm telling my mom that I'm sleeping over at Bri's house, and Bri is telling her mom that she's at mine."

Serena nods, evidently taking this very seriously. "I'll tell my mom I'm going to Bri's. She won't question it."

Colleen smirks at them. "It's so cute that you guys still have curfews."

There's a sudden tension in Serena's mouth. She throws Brianna a look and rolls her eyes. It's subtle enough to go unnoticed by Colleen.

But I notice.

Hollie joins the conversation. "What are you guys doing on Friday? Another Rook party?"

Serena takes a sip of soda before responding. "Yeah. You can come, if you want?" Her question is directed at both of us, though the glance in my direction is surely just a courtesy.

I've been to a total of two Rook parties and have zero intention of increasing that number. Hollie's been to a few more, but even she's losing interest.

Personally, I miss the Friday nights on the pier with Serena and Hollie. I miss the simpler days when it was just the three of us, hanging out at each other's houses and ordering takeout.

Hollie and I go through the motions of thanking her for the invite and telling her we'll think about it. Our words bounce off them, and the cheer girls jump into recounting tales of parties gone by.

"Ohmygod," Brianna laughs in a breath, "Scotch was so funny last weekend! Did you see him with that fire extinguisher?"

The others splutter with laughter at the seemingly hilarious anecdote.

"But Max's response was the best," Colleen says. "With the hose! He's such a chill guy. Seriously."

Imogen grins. "Max is so funny. You found a good one, Serena."

Serena smiles fondly. She opens her mouth to agree, but Colleen jumps in first. "Yeah, plus he's hot!"

Suddenly, Serena's gaze doesn't look quite so dreamy anymore.

ADAM

I fall in stride with Max as he's crossing the courtyard.

"So, go on," I say under my breath. "Tell me."

"Tell you what?"

"You know something."

He glances over his shoulder before answering. "What are you talking about?" His voice is lowered now, too.

"I've been thinking about it, trying to figure it out. The way you've been acting…"

His pace quickens, but I keep on beat with him.

"You're too happy about this Preston girl taking the heat over Colleen."

He laughs. "Yeah, I'm happy, dumbass. Because this means that nobody's gonna be looking into us. It's all on their own home turf now."

"Come on, Max. This is me you're talking to." I press my hand to my chest, right over my heart. "You can tell me. I got you."

He grimaces.

"Why are you so worried about the cops looking into us?" I press. "If you've got nothing to hide…"

A cloud moves across the sun, casting a shadow over the courtyard. Max's eyes harden.

"I don't know what you're talking about, Adam."

I meet his stare. "Yeah, you do."

"Alright, say whatever you've gotta say." He extends his arms wide. He wants me to take my best shot.

So, I do. "Did you do it? Did you kill her?"

"No."

"What happened to her?"

The muscles in his jaw clench. "I don't know."

"Come on, man. You can tell me. You know you can tell me."

But he doesn't respond. He bows his head and keeps walking.

JENNA

Kate is on the sofa when I come downstairs. Paper documents are fanned out across the coffee table, and her eyes are glued to her laptop.

I tap my fingers on the door frame to catch her attention. She looks up from the computer screen, then lowers it a little.

"Hi, hon." Her eyebrows draw together. "Are you going somewhere?"

I brush a piece of lint from the sleeve of my jacket. "Is it okay if I go out tonight? Colleen's mom has organized a vigil on the pier, and I was hoping I could go."

Kate closes her laptop completely. "Oh. Yeah, sure. I heard about that. You want me to come with you?"

"No, it's okay. I can go with Serena and a couple of her friends from the cheerleading squad."

"Okay." She tilts her head. "Will Serena's boyfriend be going?"

"Not as far as I know."

"Okay. You've got your cell?"

I tap my jeans pocket. "Yep."

She aims an index finger at me. "Straight there and straight back?"

"Of course."

"Stay with the group."

"I will." A car horn blares outside, right on cue. I glance toward the hallway. "That'll be Serena."

Kate gives me a thumbs-up. "Don't be home too late, okay?"

"I won't."

She's already reopening her laptop as I head for the door.

Outside, the day has dulled. The sky has turned golden, and the lampposts are throwing long shadows across the street. In the distance, I can see a dark stretch of the ocean, lost in the low light.

Serena's Porsche is idling alongside the curb. It's been a while since I've seen her car pulled up outside my house. It seems like a lifetime has passed since Serena, Hollie, and I last headed out for late-night frozen yogurt on the pier. Serena always drove, Hollie always picked the music, and I was in charge of getting everyone's butts off the couch.

Now, Serena's in the driver's seat, but Imogen is in the front choosing the music, and Brianna is in my old spot in the back.

I pace down the driveway and slide into the back seat next to Bri. And, just like that, I've slipped through the cracks in the dimensions and landed smack dab into their world. No longer am I heading out for frozen yogurt with Serena and Hollie, now I'm in Imogen and Brianna's version of reality. This is how they cruise around Gardiners Bay. This is how they drive to and from school every day, sipping their takeout coffees. Only today, in the perfume-and-cigarette-smoke haze, Brianna isn't sipping Starbucks, she has a bottle of Schnapps in her bubblegum-pink-polished fingers.

Brianna greets me with an air kiss. She sweeps her auburn bangs to the side and brings the bottle to her lips. On the seat beside her is a plastic bag crammed full of tealights and church candles. Paraphernalia for the vigil, I guess.

Serena catches my eye in the rearview mirror as she veers out onto the road. "I'm so glad you came tonight, Jenna. I think it's important we all show up for this."

Brianna gives me an overly enthusiastic smile.

"We need to send a message," Serena carries on. "To whoever did this, we're not afraid. We'll come out in force."

There's a beat of silence as we all try to muster confidence in the statement. Silence as we try to pretend like we're not afraid that what happened to Colleen might happen to us.

"How's Hollie?" Imogen asks. She's fiddling with the end of her platinum fishtail braid, craning her neck to glance at me from the front passenger seat.

The timing of her question makes me sit up straighter. So much for giving Hollie the benefit of the doubt.

"She's okay."

"Does she know about tonight?" Serena asks.

"She knows," I tell them. "But she wasn't up for it."

"I was going to text her," Serena adds, finding my gaze in the mirror, "but I didn't know if it would be appropriate for her to come, given the circumstances."

My shoulders tense. I can't help but feel defensive at the remark. "Hollie's got a lot on her mind right now," I say, tightly. "Besides, I don't think she'd feel comfortable going tonight, considering the way everyone's been treating her lately." I didn't specifically say their names, but Brianna's and Imogen's eyes move away from me.

I gaze out the Porsche's window at the lamplit street as we head toward the waterfront.

"Jenna?" Serena's dark eyes reflect in the mirror as she glances into the back seat. "Are you okay?"

"Mm-hmm."

"I hope tonight isn't going to be too much for you," she says. "I mean, you were the one who found her and every-thing."

I think of Adam, and the tormented look on his face as he tried to resuscitate Colleen. The quick rasps of his breath as he pressed the heels of his hands to her heart, trying to bring her back to life.

"I was just there." My voice sounds hoarse. "It was Adam who found her."

"Yeah. Max says Adam's still pretty screwed up about it."

"And how is Max doing?" The question slips from my lips. "He was close with Colleen, wasn't he?"

I swear, I feel the atmosphere in the car change.

"They weren't close," Serena says tightly. "She just used to tag along with us to Rookwood sometimes. I told you that already, remember?"

Brianna combs her fingers through her auburn waves. "Yeah, Colleen was always super flirty with the boys. Even though she knew Serena was hooking up with Max—"

Serena jumps in again. "I'm not *hooking up* with Max. We're in a relationship. There's a difference, Bri."

"Alright. We get it, Serena."

I catch Brianna rolling her eyes to Imogen. Maybe Bri

and Imogen aren't quite as adoring of Serena as I'd thought. Maybe their adoration is more toward what she can offer them—namely, an invite to Rookwood.

Serena drums her fingernails on the steering wheel as we approach a stoplight. "After graduation, Max and I are getting an apartment together." She glances at Imogen, who makes a noise of approval. "I can't wait to decorate. I've got so many cute ideas."

Imogen holds her gaze as we idle at the traffic light. "Mmm."

"I really want a place that looks out over the water. Maybe in the port."

"Wait." I lean forward in my seat. "You're buying an apartment in Gardiners Bay? What about college?"

"I'm not going." Her reply is too easy.

"Since when? I thought you were applying to UCLA?" Going to school in California had always been Serena's dream. Back when we used to hang out, I lost many hours listening to her fantasize about living in Malibu and pledging Kappa Kappa Whatever.

"College doesn't seem important anymore. Max and I want to start our lives together."

"You're seventeen! What's the rush?"

She frowns at me in the mirror. "You don't understand, Jenna. Max needs me. He needs stability."

My lips part in disbelief. "What, so you're just going to hang around Gardiners Bay doing nothing?"

"No, not nothing. I'm going to take a gap year. Max and I will go on my senior trip together, and then we're probably going to help out at my dad's company. Max wants to get involved in the business side of things."

"You've only known the guy for six months, Serena."

She glances at me. "Jenna, what's your problem?"

Fortunately, Imogen intervenes before my head explodes. "Guys, do we really need to discuss this right now? We're on our way to Colleen's vigil. Show some respect."

Brianna stares awkwardly down at her Schnapps bottle.

I drop the subject and slump back into my seat.

ADAM

"I don't think this is a good idea."

Max gives me a look. "Relax. We're just here for the vigil. Same as everyone else."

The pier is busier than I've ever seen it, crowded with people holding candles. I'm watching them, strangers, all here to mourn Colleen.

I recognize a few of the Preston girls, with their expensive coats and curious stares.

"I don't want to get seen here," I mutter.

Max's focus stays trained on the gathering of mourners. Voices are getting louder.

I grimace. "There are too many people."

Max turns to me. "Adam, chill. I just want to see what people are thinking. I want to know what they're saying. It would look worse if we didn't show."

"But we didn't know her." Even I'm starting to believe that line now.

"Come on, man. The cops know I did. Someone's given my name. Now shut the fuck up and act normal."

A blonde girl walks past us, and his eyes follow her. I recognize her from parties at the cabin.

"Hey," she says as she passes.

A shadow of a smile crosses Max's face.

I smack his arm. "At least pretend like you're not checking that girl out."

His focus snaps back to me. "I wasn't checking her out. She's one of Serena's friends."

"That didn't stop you when it was Colleen."

He doesn't respond.

I notice Serena crossing the boardwalk. It makes me wonder, did she ever pick up on the way Max and Colleen used to laugh together? Or sip from each other's drinks? Or sit closely on the couch, talking late into the night?

And then I see Jenna, and I forget why I care.

Max sees her too. And I remember again.

JENNA

It's strange being here with so many faces in the brewing dusk, all gathered in Colleen's memory. Everywhere I look, there are small candle flames flickering, dancing in the breeze. There are girls from Preston, parents, and dozens of faces I don't recognize, all huddled together at the moonlit waterfront.

Serena, Brianna, and Imogen are knotted together with their candles. I stay close to them.

Mrs. O'Dell approaches me. She takes my hand. "Jenna, isn't it?" she says. There are tears glistening in her eyes. "Thank you for coming."

My mind jumps back to that day, to the memory of Colleen's mom hurrying down to the pebbled beach. The memory of Detective Felton comforting her while she sobbed.

"I'm so sorry for your loss," I whisper.

She squeezes my hand, then steps away, swallowed by the mass of people rallying around her.

The air is cool as it drifts through the harbor. I listen as some of the girls hold their candles high and utter inspirational words about Colleen.

"We'll be thinking of you always, Colleen."

"You're our angel now."

"Rest easy, babe."

The words seem to prickle the air. It makes me shiver. Everything about this night makes me shiver.

Mrs. O'Dell is crying into a tissue, and Mr. O'Dell has his arm around her.

I turn to Serena, but her attention has drifted elsewhere. I follow her gaze. In the shadows, I see them. Max and Adam.

Suddenly, my phone vibrates, making me jump. *Hollie* lights up the screen.

I answer immediately. "Hol?"

Shattered breaths echo through the line. "Jenna. It's really bad."

I step away from the crowd and press my hand over my other ear. "What happened?"

"The police want me to go into the station tomorrow." Her words are punctuated by hiccupping sobs. "My lawyer thinks they're going to arrest me."

My breath escapes in a rush. "Oh, my god. Is this about those stupid text messages?" I hold my cell close to my ear and head toward the harbor, where it's quieter.

"And there's something else. Something to do with the handprints." Her words are fractured.

"The handprints?"

"On Colleen's throat," she manages. "I don't know what they found, but my lawyer thinks it's bad news. Evidence that could implicate me somehow."

An image flashes through my mind. Bruises on Colleen's throat. I squeeze my eyes shut and force it away.

"I didn't do it, Jenna! I swear, I didn't do it."

"Oh, Hollie," I murmur. "I'm so sorry."

"I didn't do it."

I can barely pick out the words through her tears.

My throat feels tight, all of a sudden. "What can I do? How can I help?"

"You can't. I'm going to prison, Jenna."

"No, you're not. I can help. I can be a character witness. I can—"

"You can't do anything. I've got to go," she chokes. "I can't."

The line goes dead.

I try calling her back, but it's sent to voice mail after the first ring.

My heart starts racing. I glance over my shoulder. I'm alone, invisible to the people congregated on the pier. To them, I'm probably just a shadow moving among the sailboats and yachts.

The cold air bites at my hands as I open the saved images on my phone and search for the picture I took of Max's transcript. I skim over it again. He gives nothing away, and yet he's clearly on edge. Surely, he wouldn't have been interviewed without good reason. The investigators chose *him* out of all the Rooks that Colleen partied with. There has to be more to it than chance.

Maybe you should ask her friends.

From what I can gauge of Max, he's not naïve. He must have known that a comment like that is suggestive. He was

being backed into a corner, and he was ready to sell someone out to save his own ass.

"Serena?" I pace across the harbor through pools of lamp-
light, to where a group has branched off and gathered in the
shadows behind the locked clubhouse.

"Hey, Jenna!"

I step a little closer. I can see Serena now. Brianna and
Imogen are with her. Max and Adam are there, too. They've
formed a semicircle, sitting on the paved floor. None of them
know about my call with Hollie, and I don't plan on telling
them, either.

"Where've you been?" Serena asks. She gives me an easy
smile. A smile that's not at all in sync with the tone of tonight.

"I've been talking to Mrs. O'Dell. Everything's wrapping
up now." I cast a glance back to the pier. It's pretty much de-
serted as people head back to their cars en masse. A few candles have been discarded. Some of the flames still sway with
the breeze, while others are snuffed out. "Are you guys ready
to go?" I don't look at Max when I speak, but I can sure as
hell feel him looking at me.

"Oh." Serena's face falls. "Actually, Jenna, we were thinking of moving the party to Rookwood."

"Party?" I echo. "Since when was this a party?"

Brianna raises a bottle of vodka and shakes it. "Since we
got this."

It's only then that I notice the slur in their words.

Awesome. My designated driver is wasted.

"When did you get that?"

The girls giggle.

"Max stole it from the store," Brianna tells me.

Serena flaps her hands. "Shh!"

They giggle again.

My gaze flickers to Max. He's smirking. Adam is staring down at the pavement.

"You should come to Rookwood with us," Imogen says to me. "Party with us."

"I don't think so." My eyes skate over Max again. "I've got to get home. I'll see you guys on Monday."

"Wait, Jenna!" Serena calls. "You can't walk home alone. I'll give you a ride." She stands, wobbles, then falls back into Max's lap and shrieks with laughter.

"I'm good," I tell her. "I'll call Kate. And I don't think you should drive yourself home tonight, either."

Another round of giggles.

I start making my way back across the harbor, stepping through the pools of light. My footsteps echo on beat with the squeals of tipsy laughter. I text Kate an SOS message, and she replies, On my way.

While I wait for Kate to show, I take a seat on one of the boardwalk benches and stare out at the water. Alone, with only the distant sound of voices, I think about Colleen. I wonder if she ever sat on this very bench and gazed out at the water just like I'm doing now. I wonder what went through her mind on that night as she made her way home from Rookwood.

Was she happy? Sad? Angry?

My thoughts wander to Hollie. Everything has spiraled so fast. What possible evidence could they have on her? Other than the text messages.

I remember the bruises on Colleen's throat. The finger marks...

Somebody sits beside me on the bench, and I jump.

"I saw you come over here." Adam's voice is careful. "I thought you might want some company."

I inhale slowly. "Oh. Thanks. Don't you have to go back to Rookwood with the others?"

"I'll catch up with them." He hesitates. "Are you alright?"

"Yeah. It's just that tonight was..."

"Intense?"

"Yeah," I murmur.

I follow his gaze to the ocean. The sounds of the harbor bounce around the night, the clunking buoys and the tide sloshing beneath the jetties.

"I lied to you the other day."

I turn to him, studying his profile as I wait for him to continue. His caramel-colored eyes are still locked on the water. A few strands of his brown hair are stirred by the night breeze.

"I did know Colleen."

I dip my gaze. "I know you did."

"That picture," he says. "The one that was taken at the cabin, the last time Colleen was at Rookwood. I remember that night. I remember her."

"That was the night she died."

"I know." He gives way to a long breath. "I just keep thinking, maybe I could have done something. If I'd followed her. When she left, I should have gone after her. I should have checked that she made it back to wherever she was going. If I'd have just gone after her, I could have done something to stop this."

I get it now. When he said this before, on the beach, he didn't mean CPR or some abstract *If only I'd arrived sooner*. He meant it literally. He thinks he could have intervened.

"Hey." I draw his focus to me. "You can't blame yourself for that. You can't go following every person home, just in case."

"I know. But I should have. I could have."

"Adam…"

He stares down at his sneakers.

Just in case. But it's not a hypothetical.

There's something more. Something he's still not saying.

I swallow. This is my chance. I know it is.

For Hollie.

"I know about Max," I say. "Serena told me." My gaze shifts from him. I can't look at him, mostly because I'm afraid that if he sees my eyes he'll somehow see the lie at the heart of my vague comment.

"What do you mean?" His voice has changed. His tone is rigid now, weighted with tension.

"Serena told me everything."

His words come out fast. "She knew?"

I drag my gaze back to him. His lips are parted, and his eyes are darting between me and the water.

"Colleen told Serena?" he presses.

I catch my breath as a breeze slithers through the harbor and ripples the water. What could Colleen have told Serena about Max? What did Colleen know?

"I think so," I manage.

"She must have," Adam mutters. "Colleen threatened Max that night. I think he was trying to end it with her or something, but Colleen lost it and said she was going to tell Serena everything."

My stomach does flips.

Suddenly, his eyes cloud. Clearly, my expression was enough to give away my shock. To give away my lies.

A wave of guilt floods over me.

He gropes for words. "No. I mean…"

It's too late for either of us to regain our composure. It's all unraveled. For both of us.

Adam jumps up from the bench and cusses under his breath.

I stare down at my hands.

"You didn't know anything, did you?" His voice has turned cold.

"I'm sorry," I murmur. It's all I can think to say. Not that it means much now.

He rubs his hands over his face.

"Max was cheating on Serena with Colleen," I say, piecing it together. "And Colleen threatened to tell Serena. But she didn't get to Serena. Because someone stopped her."

Adam's chest is rising and falling fast.

"No prizes for guessing who stopped her."

His breathing starts to sound ragged. "Max didn't go after Colleen, if that's what you're thinking."

"That's exactly what I'm thinking."

"You're wrong."

"So, what? Colleen threatens him, then winds up dead, and it's just a coincidence?"

"I didn't say it was a coincidence." He holds my gaze in the moonlight. "All I said was, Max didn't do it."

"Then tell me who did?"

"I don't know. How about the person whose boyfriend cheated on her?"

I stare back at him, numb.

"Maybe no one stopped Colleen," he carries on. "Maybe she *did* do what she'd set out to do."

It takes me a second to follow his train of thought. I shake my head as he says her name aloud.

"Serena."

Interview with Serena Blake,
conducted by Detective Kate Dallas at 10:30 a.m.
on Tuesday, October 2nd.

K.D.: Hi, Serena. How are you?

S.B.: Not good, Kate. I'm so sad about everything. I feel sick just thinking about it. Poor Colleen.

K.D.: I'm sorry, Serena. I appreciate how tough this must be for you.

S.B.: Thanks. How's Jenna?

K.D.: Serena, tell me about your friendship with Colleen O'Dell.

S.B.: We were good friends. She was on the squad.

K.D.: To clarify, the cheerleading squad?

S.B.: Yes. I'm captain. Colleen got asked to hand in her uniform a little while back, though.

K.D.: Colleen got kicked off the team? Why?

S.B.: To be honest with you, Kate—I mean, Detective Dallas—she was slacking. Also, she was flunking a couple of classes, and some people were saying she was smoking pot. Not me, just people were saying it. I heard.

K.D.: So, she was cut from the team?

S.B.: Miss Keeley cut her. Not me.

K.D.: Would you say you spent a lot of time with Colleen, outside of cheerleading?

S.B.: Not really.

K.D.: But, you were friends?

S.B.: Yes, but not close friends.

K.D.: Some of your classmates are saying Colleen spent quite a bit of time with the Rookwood students. Serena? Are you okay?

S.B.: Yes. I'm fine.

K.D.: You're dating one of the boys from Rookwood, Max. Is that right?

S.B.: Yes. Max and I are in a relationship.

K.D.: Max and Colleen were friends, yes?

S.B.: No. She used to tell people they were friends—you know, for status—but they never hung out or anything.

K.D.: So, they weren't friends?

S.B.: No. Definitely not.

K.D.: Right. Thanks for clearing that up for me, Serena.

S.B.: No problem, Kate. I'm glad I could help.

ADAM

I watch her from across the room.

Serena.

Her dark eyes are following Max. She reminds me of an oil painting, with that hollow stare tracking him wherever he goes.

He's aware of her, too. It's not as obvious, but I see it. He's leaning against the cabin doorway, looking almost relaxed. There's an unlit cigarette bobbing between his lips as he laughs, but he glances her way every now and then. That's how I know he's aware of her eyes on him.

He's talking to a blonde girl in the doorway, and she's laughing along with him. She offers him a light. He bows his head toward the flame. His eyes skate over Serena as the end of the cigarette glows red-hot.

The Preston girls haven't been coming here that long. A couple of weeks, maybe. Ever since Max and Serena first hooked up, she and her crew have spilled over into our world. They've taken up residency at the cabin, showing up every Friday night and staying until the sun comes up.

But I don't know them. And they don't know me.

I take a seat beside Serena on the couch, and she flinches. She didn't see me coming.

"Hi. Adam, isn't it?"

"Yeah. You're Serena, right?"

She nods.

"You okay?"

Her eyebrows pull together. "Of course. Why wouldn't I be?"

"I don't know. I just thought you looked…"

"What?"

I shrug.

"I'm fine." She presses the rim of her beer bottle to her lips and knocks it back hard.

"Good."

An awkward silence hangs between us. I stare at the wall. She stares at her bottle.

"She a friend of yours?" I ask, nodding toward the open doorway.

Her gaze flickers across the room and lands on Max and the blonde girl. They're still laughing as they pass the cigarette back and forth between them. His lips to hers, then back again.

Serena drags her focus back to me. "Yeah. We go to school together."

"She and Max look close."

Her eyes harden. "What do you mean by that?"

"Nothing." I hold up my hands. "I was just saying."

Her teeth clench beneath her red lipstick. I think she's trying to smile. "Max and I are dating," she says. "We're exclusive."

I swallow a laugh.

She straightens her slender shoulders. "Max and I are good."

"Good."

"He's allowed to have female friends, y'know?"

"I know."

Her mouth presses into a tight line. "He's not interested in anyone else."

"Okay."

She thinks she's got him down. But she doesn't know him. Not really. She doesn't know how he self-destructs. He wants to self-destruct. I see it in him. He thrives off the rush of his own downfall.

Serena doesn't know that.

Serena doesn't know him.

And I wouldn't want to be around when she figures that out.

The night breeze stirs her chestnut-brown hair.

Forget I said anything. That's what I want to tell her.

But it's too late. I know it's too late. I messed up, I let my guard down, and now Jenna knows about Max and Colleen.

I move to walk away, but she stops me.

"I'm sorry," she says again. I can see it in her eyes. She's telling the truth. This wasn't about me. It wasn't about playing me. It was about her friend Hollie.

I can't blame her. I'd have done the same thing if Tommy's or Max's necks were on the line. Rules don't apply when you're looking out for your own.

I run my hand over my mouth. "You should think about what I said." My voice gets lost in the darkness. "My money's on her. Serena. I think Serena killed Colleen."

Jenna shakes her head. "You're wrong."

"It wasn't Max. He said he didn't do it, and I believe him. I think he knows something, though. He's protecting Serena. That's what I think."

She breathes out a laugh. "You've got to be kidding. Max has motive. *He*'s the shady one, not Serena. She has no idea that he's been cheating on her!"

"Or maybe she's a good liar."

Jenna squeezes her eyes shut for a second, probably wishing she didn't know any of this. It's a wish we share.

But I'm not done. "You think it too, don't you? There's a part of you that questions Serena."

"No. Of course not. Serena is my friend."

"And Max is my friend."

We fall silent. The sounds from the group across the harbor leak out into the night. They're leaving now, heading toward Rookwood. The world is still turning around us. I want it to stop, rewind.

"I have to tell Serena about Max and Colleen," Jenna says. "She has a right to know what they were doing behind her back."

"She already knows," I mutter. "Because Colleen told her. Weeks ago."

"I—"

"And now Colleen's dead."

She scowls back at me. "Yes. Colleen is dead because she threatened Max."

"No. I was with Max that night," I say, pressing my hand to my heart. "I was there when Colleen went off on him. Colleen left, and Max didn't go after her. He went outside the cabin. He talked on his phone, then he came back inside. That was it."

She shivers as my words sink in. "I don't believe you."

"It's the truth."

"Who was he talking to? When he went outside, who did he call?"

"I don't know. Probably Colleen, asking her to stop. Or maybe Serena. Maybe he wanted to come clean before Colleen busted him."

She's breathing fast now. "What about after? You can't have been with him all night. He must have left your sight at some point."

I don't respond. She's right, though.

It *could* have been Max, just as easily as it *could* have been Serena. Hell, it could have been Tommy.

It could have been me.

Jenna's voice brings me back to her. "Serena would have told me, if she knew."

A rasp of breath escapes me. "Sure, she'd tell you if she offed Colleen, watching as she struggled—"

"She'd have told me if Max was cheating on her." Abruptly, Jenna stands up from the bench.

An SUV pulls up alongside the curb. The driver's window rolls down.

My chest tightens. It's the cop. Detective Dallas.

"Kate," Jenna says, and my heart starts beating faster. Of course. Jenna's aunt is the cop. "This is my friend," she fumbles. "Adam. I think you've met."

The cop eyeballs me. "Yes. Adam Cole. Hello again."

I mutter some dumbass response, before getting out of there. Fast.

I just screwed Max over, big-time.

JENNA

I stare out the car window as Kate drives us home.

My mind is a complete jumble of thoughts—and none of them are good.

"So, Adam?" Kate's voice makes me jump. "A friend of yours, is he?"

Kate's not dumb, she knows exactly who Adam is.

"Not really. He's a friend of Serena's boyfriend."

"Right. The Rookwood boy."

"Mmm."

She taps her fingers on the steering wheel. "Were you guys drinking tonight?"

I resist the urge to roll my eyes. "No, Kate. They were. I left."

"Oh. Well, I'm glad you called me. Thank you for that."

"You see? Turns out I am responsible, after all. Go figure."

She glances at me and smiles. "I always knew you were responsible, Jenna."

A knot tightens in my stomach. If I was responsible, I'd blurt out everything Adam told me. But the cost would be implicating Serena in a homicide investigation. Yet, this could be exactly the kind of evidence Hollie needs to get out of this mess.

One thing's for sure, I have to talk to Serena first. She needs to hear this from me, not from some investigator showing up on her doorsteps with an arrest warrant.

I slip my phone from my jacket pocket. The screen beams out at me, a glaring contrast to the dark car. I type a message to Serena, telling her everything, about Max cheating on her with Colleen and Colleen threatening Max on the night she died. Everything.

Then I delete it.

I try again, going simpler this time. Just a, *Hey. We need to talk. Call me when you get this.*

I almost hit send. But I can't do it.

Telling Serena about Max and Colleen will destroy her. As far as Serena is concerned, she and Max are solid. She loves him, and I'm about to totally blindside her. I can't do that over a text message. I can't even do that with a vague, mysterious "we need to talk" text.

If I'm about to ruin her life, I should at least do it in person.

This *will* blindside her. Adam is wrong. There's no way Serena could have known about Max's cheating and covered it up. She's completely besotted by the guy. She defends his character with the conviction of someone who truly believes her own words. They're not the words of someone who's been cheated on.

In my opinion, Max is the only person who had something to gain from Colleen's death. He had something to hide. He had something to lose. Namely, her dad's empire and a swanky prepaid apartment to boot. Max was protecting himself.

And now I have to protect Serena.

ADAM

It's a while before I can face going back to Rookwood. By the time I arrive, it's pitch-black in the forest. The cabin is a beacon of light, alive with music and voices. Max and Tommy must have spread the word, because some of the other guys have joined from the dorms.

Inside, the room is humid, full of bodies, all moving slower than they had been before. It's as though they're underwater. Their eyes are bleary and unfocused as they drag their limbs through the motions, all drunk off stolen beers and spirits.

Max is standing at the bar. He's sloppy. There's a plastic cup in his hand, and beer is sloshing over the sides as he talks with some of the guys. I can't see Serena anywhere, but one of her friends is still here. She's dancing on the pool table, her long braid swaying from side to side as her bangs fall over her face.

Silently, I cross the room and pat Max on the shoulder. I gesture for him to follow me, and he does. We step outside and skirt around to the back of the cabin.

Once we're out of sight, he stops walking.

It's quieter here, with only the groan of wind and the thump of bass music leaking through the log walls.

Max's jaw clenches as he tries to read my expression. "What?" A simple word.

"Something happened. I messed up."

"Tell me."

"Someone was asking about Colleen tonight."

He presses his knuckles to his mouth. "Who?"

"A girl from Preston."

His eyes narrow. "Yeah. And?"

"She knows about you cheating on Serena."

He sucks in his lower lip. "How? Colleen told her?"

"*I* told her."

He takes a step backward like I punched him in the gut. I feel the impact too. I swear, I feel it just as bad.

I was supposed to have his back.

I wait for him to say something.

"What the fuck is wrong with you, man?" he hisses. "Why would you do that to me?"

"I thought she knew." I scrub my hands through my hair. "I messed up. I thought she already knew."

He glances along the path that leads back to the cabin's entrance. "Does Serena know?" His voice is low.

"You don't have to cover for her," I tell him. "She already knows, doesn't she? You told her, and she went after Colleen."

"No!"

"Max." I try again. "Come on. You can tell me. That night, you called her, didn't you? After Colleen left, you went outside, and you called Serena."

He slams his palm into the wall. "*No.*"

I'd expected him to look awkward when I confronted him. To mumble out a feeble response, and then I'd know for sure that all this time he's been covering for Serena. Serena killed Colleen, and Max knew about it all along.

But he just keeps staring at me like I've lost it.

"I'm right, though, aren't I?" Tell me I'm right.

"No. That didn't happen."

I drop my voice. "You're not covering for Serena? Swear to me right now that you're not covering for her."

"No! Serena doesn't know shit!"

My skin prickles in the cold night air. "How do you know? Because you got to Colleen first?"

I watch his eyes. His focus shifts from me to the forest, then back again. There's tension in his jaw. He's lying to me. He knows more than he's saying.

My words come out fast. "You did it."

He squares up to me. I brace myself for his fist to swing. I figure I probably have it coming. But the punch isn't directed at me. He throws it at the wall instead. In the moonlight, I see the skin on his knuckles split open and blood spill onto his hand.

"I thought I could trust you, Adam."

I grab his shoulder. "You can."

"You sold me out," he spits, and he pushes me away.

There's nothing I can say. It's true.

"Who's the girl?" he rasps. "Which one of the Preston girls did you tell?"

I keep my voice steady. "I don't know her name."

"What do you mean, you don't know her name? You've

got time to tell her my business, but you don't have time to ask her goddamn name?"

I grit my teeth. "Like I said, I don't know."

His mouth crooks into a smile. "Oh." He draws out the word. "I get it."

"What?"

"It was *her*. Jenna, is it? Is that her name?"

I shake my head.

"Jenna." He says her name again, and I don't like the way it sounds on his lips. "Is she here?"

"She's not here."

"Then where is she?"

"I don't know."

"Bullshit." He sucks a breath through his teeth. "I'll just have to go find her, then. How about that?"

Blood pumps fast through my veins. He's threatening me. He's found a weakness—a weakness I didn't even know I had.

I breathe slowly. "Yeah. You could go find her. But then I'd have to come find you."

He runs his thumb over his mouth, barely noticing the blood smeared across the back of his hand.

We're both backed into a corner. One of us will break. One of us has to. But it won't be me.

"Colleen's dead," I carry on, "and I heard what she said to you that night. I was there. Then she disappears, shows up dead."

"You're calling me a murderer?" His breathing is fast. He's getting scared.

"Colleen was coming for you that night, Max. She was mad as hell."

"Yeah, because the girl was obsessed with me."

"Exactly. She was coming for you. So, if you didn't tell Serena…"

"Hey." He cuts me off. "I'm not the only one Colleen took a pop at that night. How about Tommy? You saw the look on his face when Colleen said she knew his secret. She was ready to bust him as a dealer. He would have been done."

"Tommy wouldn't kill anyone."

"Oh, but I would?" He slaps his palm to his chest. "How about you? Maybe you killed her. We all know you have violent tendencies. We all know that." His teeth are bared as he talks.

My fists ball. I know exactly what he's referring to.

"Don't," I warn him. "Don't go there."

His jaw tenses, and he rubs the nape of his neck. "I don't want to fight with you, man. I don't want it to be this way."

"Neither do I."

He looks down at the ground.

"Truth," I murmur. "Do you know what happened to Colleen?"

There's a long beat of silence between us, and then he nods.

My chest tightens, as if the air has been knocked right out of me. I thought I was prepared for this. But seeing him admit it, after all this time, after all these lies, it catches me off guard. It shouldn't. But it does.

The earth feels insubstantial beneath my feet. "Was it you?"

The sound of muffled voices and crunching leaves makes us both stop. We freeze, eyes searching the darkness.

"Who's back there?" Max yells.

We pace around the corner of the cabin.

I recognize Tommy right away, shaggy black hair tousled by the night breeze. There's someone else with him, a guy I don't recognize. *A drug deal*, that's my first thought. It takes me a moment to register that they're both shirtless, jeans un-buttoned, hands moving quickly over bare skin.

Max steps on a twig, and the cracking sound makes Tommy jump back from the other guy like he's been burned. Tommy's face drops when he sees us.

"No." He gropes for words. "This isn't…"

The wind drags through the trees.

Tommy grabs his clothes from the ground. He sidles past us, fumbling with his shirt buttons as he goes.

I take off after him, but he disappears into the blackness of the tangled forest.

"Tommy?" I call.

My voice echoes back at me as I stand alone in the darkness.

I open the dorm room door and stop.

Tommy's sitting on the floor with his knees bent up to his chest. His hands are knotted through his hair.

He flinches when he sees me.

"Hey." I slip my headphones down around my neck. "You okay?"

He forces a smile. "Yeah. I thought you had class."

"I did. It was canceled. There was a Code Red." I watch his eyes. He won't hold my gaze. He drops his hands, and his fingers thread together, gnawed thumbnails pressing into the skin on his palms. "What's wrong?"

He jumps up from the floor and straightens out his t-shirt. "Noth-ing," he mumbles. "I gotta…" He doesn't finish the sentence, he's al-ready halfway across the room, sidestepping me on his way to the door.

"Hey." I stop him. "What's wrong?"

He shakes his head. His eyes are bloodshot, watery.

"Tommy. Talk to me."

He bites down on his lip. "Colleen…"

I wait.

He draws in a breath. "She had so much dirt on us, Adam. What if she'd already told people?"

"She said she knew your secret. So, what? It was an empty threat. She had no proof that you were dealing, and she wouldn't have gone to the cops anyway. It was all talk."

He swallows.

"And even if it does get out," I add, "we'll cover for you. We'll pin it all on Scotch." It's a joke, but Tommy doesn't smile.

"It wasn't just the dealing. Colleen had more on me than that."

"Yeah?" I wait for him to continue. But he doesn't. "Tommy?"

"I can't. I want to. I just can't."

The door falls shut behind him.

"It's okay," I mutter into the empty room. "I already know."

ADAM: Where did you go?

ADAM: Max. Pick up. Where you at?

MAX: I gotta go do something.

ADAM: Why aren't you answering my calls?

MAX: Later.

ADAM: Where are you?

ADAM: Are you looking for Jenna?

ADAM: Max?

JENNA

I wake with a start to the sound of a text message. My skin is clammy, and my heart's beating fast. In the darkness of my bedroom, I detach myself from the nightmare, the warped images of Colleen, Serena, and Max, entangled together, their hands drenched in blood.

Their bodies drenched in blood.

The weak light from the streetlamp outside spills a gentle glow into my room through the open curtains. My phone reads 2:16, and there are unread messages. Imogen's name is at the top of my screen.

Where are you? Is everything okay?

There's an older message too, from Serena this time. It was sent just after midnight.

Did you get home okay? Check in, Jenna!

I squint against the bright backlight and type out a quick response to both.

I'm home. I'm fine.

As I reach across my nightstand to close the curtains, my eyes wander to the quiet, lamplit street outside.

Breath catches in my throat.

"Kate!" My scream cuts through the silence.

There's someone out there. A silhouette in the shadows, staring up at our house.

I hear the quick thud of footsteps in the hallway. Kate rushes into my room, wrapping her robe around herself. Her eyes are puffy from sleep. "Jenna, what's wrong?"

"Someone's watching the house."

We both stare out into the night.

But there's no one there.

I lock my window and yank the curtains shut.

ADAM

My feet hit the pavement. My breath comes out in rasps. Thumps. My heart, my lungs, my sneakers on the tarmac.

I know where she is, and I get there fast. She lives in that nice suburban house near Lighthouse Point. The place with the long windows, next door to the house where the hedges are shaped like horses. In the darkness, those horses look like grizzly bears, and those long windows reflect back at me. I see myself, my ghostly reflection trapped inside the glass. I'm standing on the curb, my eyes darting up and down the quiet street.

I can't see him anywhere. But he warned me. He said he'd come looking for her.

I know him.

I just don't know what he's capable of. I don't know what I'm capable of, either.

JENNA

Kate is already in the kitchen by the time I get downstairs on Saturday morning. She has her cell pressed to her ear. There's the usual array of paperwork scattered across the island around her open laptop.

"I'm aware of that, Felton," she's saying into her phone, "but people are getting scared. Jenna thinks there was someone hanging around outside our house last night." She notices me and attempts a smile—although it's more like a grimace. "That doesn't change anything," she says into her phone. "We need those autopsy reports before revisiting the statements." She covers the mouthpiece and whispers to me, "There's coffee in the pot." Then returns to her conversation with an abrupt, "Officer Mowry wasn't on duty that day."

I slip past her and pour myself a cup of coffee.

Vainly pretending I'm not hanging off Kate's every word, I slide into a seat at the breakfast bar and check the news app on my cell. Unsurprisingly, Colleen's story is still headlining the local sector. None of the articles are calling Colleen's death a tragic accident anymore.

And between Hollie and Serena, that makes two of my closest friends potential suspects in a homicide case...not that Serena's connection is public knowledge. Yet.

Tearing my eyes away from the now familiar thumbnail picture of Colleen smiling in her Preston cheerleading uniform, I move on to my emails. There's a new message in my inbox from Mom. I open it and download the attached images. The first is a picture of Vietnam. It's a city scene, capturing the motion of pedestrians on a dusty street, oblivious to the person watching them from behind the lens.

My gaze wanders over the text in the body of the email. Hi, I miss you! Vietnam is incredible. Everything's going great, and a Cambodian magazine has picked up some of my articles from This Girl's Guide. And guess what, Jenna, I've met someone! In the second image, I see Mom with her arms wrapped around a middle-aged guy with long hair. They're grinning, content in their own little world that I'm not a part of.

I open up a reply email and type out my response. It starts off with the usual, Hi! Miss you, too, that kind of thing. And I do miss her. Of course I do—she's my mom. But it's been such a long time since I've seen her, the months and years have turned her into some abstract part of my identity. I miss the feeling of knowing what it's like to be around her. Kate is amazing, and we've got the whole niece-aunt relationship nailed, but I haven't had a "mom" in a really long time. I miss knowing what that's like.

I push the thoughts aside and carry on with my reply. That's awesome about the magazine—well done, Mom! Who's the guy?

Tell me everything! Then, before I can stop myself, words are flowing onto the screen, omitting the usual pleasantries. I need your advice. What if you had information that could save one friend at the cost of another?

What if you start to doubt the people you thought you knew best?

I look again at Mom's city photo. All of these people, just going about their day minding their own business. What the image can't possibly show is what's inside their minds. What they're thinking. What they're hiding.

Kate drops into a seat at the breakfast bar, and I jump. I quickly flip my phone facedown onto the counter.

"Morning, hon." Kate runs a hand through her wavy hair. "I'm sorry about that." She slaps her cell down beside mine and takes a long sip of coffee from her mug.

"That's okay. I didn't interrupt you, did I?"

"No, no. You're fine."

"What did Felton say?" I ask, sitting a little taller in my seat. "Have there been any developments with the investigation?"

"Not yet." She musters a weak smile. "But we're interviewing more people today."

"Hollie?"

She pats my hand. "We've still got a lot of people we need to talk to. There's a ton to get through." She gestures to the paperwork covering the breakfast bar. "Case in point."

I feel queasy, all of a sudden. I should tell her. I know I should tell her.

"Kate, I—"

Her cell starts to ring.

"One sec," she says as she pounces on her phone. "Detective Dallas speaking."

While she's distracted, I reopen the email to Mom and delete the last few sentences, leaving only the pleasantries behind. Mom can't help me with this. No one can. I need to make the call on whether or not what I know about Max and Colleen should be made public, at the cost of hurting—and possibly incriminating—Serena. I sign off the email with *x*s and *o*s and hit send.

Kate draws in a sharp breath. "When?" she says into the phone. "Where?" She pauses, then grabs her keys from the counter. "I'll be right there." She ends the call and heads for the door.

"Kate, what's wrong?" I call after her.

"There's been an incident at the harbor."

My brow creases. "What kind of incident?"

"10-54."

My heart leaps into my throat. I've heard her use that code before. Serena. Serena was at the harbor last night. Imogen and Brianna, too. I suddenly remember their predawn messages. They were checking up on me, but I didn't even think to check up on them.

Kate's voice interrupts my racing thoughts. "Another body has been found."

ADAM

I'm not a violent person.

I know that's what people say about me, that I'm dangerous, and that's why my dad sent me here. They think that coming to Rookwood was my "get out of jail free" card. If you surrender, reform, they'll let you off for murder.

But I didn't do anything.

I don't think I did, anyway.

I stare at the bleak dorm room walls. These four walls are branded with memories of all the years past, yet somehow they're still bland, devoid of any personality, anything that connects us to the lives we had before. The people we were before.

But staring at the cracks in the plaster reminds me of those first few months, when all I could do was stare.

Tommy didn't come back to the dorm last night. He took off right after Max and I found him with that guy, and he didn't come back. I waited up until dawn, expecting him to appear at some point. But he never showed.

I press dial on his number for what must be the dozenth time.

His prerecorded voice comes back to me, "Hey, this is Tommy. Leave me a message. Or not."

"It's me," I say into the phone after the beep. "I'm around, if you want to talk. Or not."

Before I toss the phone, I see a new message on my screen.

I open the text, and my pulse accelerates at the sight of Jenna's name. I don't know if that's because I want to hear from her...or not.

Hi, are you okay? That's all it says.

I type back. Yeah. Listen, about last night, did you talk to Serena?

Yes. She's fine. So are Brianna and Imogen.

I frown at the new message. So Jenna told Serena about Max and Colleen hooking up, and she and her friends are cool with it? And that isn't the sketchiest reaction?

My thumbs move over the keypad. I think we should talk. In person.

She's writing back. When? Where?

The beach, I reply. Fifteen minutes.

I slip my cell into my jeans pocket and shrug into my jacket. Outside, the air is cold, and the sky above the treetops is silver. There are a couple of cop cars parked in the campus court-yard. I keep my head bowed as I dodge past them on my way to the track leading down to the beach.

JENNA

Adam is already on the beach by the time I arrive. He's sitting on the rocks below the walkway. His short brown hair is moving in the ocean breeze, and his gaze is trained on the rippling water. The tide is choppy today, unsettled.

I climb down onto the rocks and navigate a path across the sand and pebbles.

Adam turns his attention to me. He stands. His hands are in his jacket pockets as he walks toward me, stepping over the uneven stones.

"Hi." His voice sounds tired.

"Hey." I can't help but feel relieved by the sight of him.

I'm starting to notice things about him, I realize, like how dark his lashes are and the way his mouth lifts at the corner into an almost-smile. Today, I look at him closer than I've ever done before.

There's an ease to his expression, actually. Something that makes me think he doesn't know what I know.

Suddenly, *I think we should talk* takes on a whole new meaning.

"I'm glad you texted me," he says. "I've been thinking a lot about last night."

I draw in a shallow breath.

"We're on the same side, Jenna," he tells me. "I know that might be hard for you to believe. But I mean it. I want to know what happened to Colleen just as much as you do."

The cold breeze pulls a strand of my hair free from my ponytail and whips it across my cheekbone. I push it back behind my ear and take a steadying breath. "Do you know about what's been going on at the harbor this morning?"

He frowns back at me. "What do you mean?"

I close my eyes for a second. "I'm sorry. I assumed you knew. I thought that's why you asked if I'd talked to Serena. I thought that's why you wanted to meet…"

"Knew what? What's going on?"

"Another body has been found."

His lips part. "What? What body? Whose body?"

"I don't know," I murmur. "But that's why I texted you. I was worried. I thought it might have been…"

You.

He yanks his phone from his jeans pocket and punches the buttons. The sound of a voice mail response leaks softly out into our world. *Hey, this is Tommy. Leave me a message—* Adam hangs up the call. "Are you sure? Are you sure you've got this right?"

I nod, unable to find my voice.

"I've gotta go," he mutters. "I've gotta get to the harbor."

He turns and heads across the beach. I follow after him, quickening my pace to keep up with his long strides.

"Tommy," he says. His words sound muddled. "It's Tommy.

He didn't come back to our room last night. I should have gone looking for him. I knew I should have…"

"Stop. You don't know it's him." I want to comfort him, touch him, take his hand, anything, but he's tense as we scramble quickly over the rocks.

We climb up to the boardwalk and race along the promenade. Eventually, the harbor comes into view. It's the same sight I looked out over last night, only from the opposite angle. A mirror reflection. Except everything's brighter in daylight. The colors aren't muted anymore.

Just above the beach, we stand, staring. Police and forensics are already swarming the place, wearing white jumpsuits as they scan the ground. Kate is a little farther away, talking to two cops in uniform.

There's a car attached to a tow truck. It's being held at the edge of the jetty, still glistening with water as if it's just been dredged up. Some members of the white-suited forensic team are dusting the interior for prints.

I hold my breath, staying beside Adam on the outskirts.

"Whose car is that?" I whisper.

His breath comes out fast. "It's mine."

A sky-blue Dodge pulls up into one of the spaces in the pier parking lot.

*Serena's attention snaps away from Hollie and me. "Oh my god,"
she breathes. "Rooks."*

I peer over the top of my latte and across Chai's deck. I hold my cup to my lips for a moment while my gaze lingers on the car in the neighboring lot.

The engine stops running, and the bass music cuts out. The boys'
voices drift from the open window. They're laughing loudly.

I recognize the boy in the driver's seat, and I stop myself from
staring.

It's the guy from the beach. The guy who'd been swimming at
dawn. The guy I've been thinking about for the past couple of weeks.

It hits me, and my stomach knots. He's a Rook.

Suddenly, Serena starts laughing.

I frown at her.

She notches up the volume of her giggle, flipping her hair too.
She's peacocking. Totally.

Hollie joins in.

I raise an eyebrow.

Hollie grins at me and shrugs.

"Unbelievable," I mutter, shaking my head.

The three boys are out of the car now and heading toward the mar-
ket. They didn't even glance this way—much to Serena's and Hol-
lie's disappointment.

"Oh my god," Serena whispers. "They're so hot." She starts fan-
ning her face with a napkin. "I'm obsessed."

I snatch the napkin from her hand. "Yeah. Why, exactly? You
don't even know these guys."

"Exactly. That's the point."

"The mystique," Hollie adds. "They're like mythical beings who
only venture out on a full moon."

I glance up at the cloudless blue sky, where the April sun beats
down on the rippling ocean.

"Or on bright, sunny days," Hollie says, following my gaze. "Se-
mantics."

Serena's attention is still on the market doorway—the portal that stole the boys. "I just had the best idea." She drags her gaze back to Hollie and me. "This is our opportunity to get in with the Rooks. The gods have presented us with a gift, a rare sighting, and we can't waste it, ladies. We have to talk to them."

"We don't know them," I remind her. "What are we going to talk to them about?"

"I don't know. Whatever. Anything. We just need them to hang out with us."

"They don't want to hang out with us," I say. "They have their own thing going on."

She gasps at the insult. "Of course they'll want to hang out with us! Don't be such a naysayer, Jenna. We're three hot girls. They're three hot guys." She slaps her hands together. "It's basic math."

Hollie leans back in her seat and raises an index finger. "I call dibs on the blond."

"You can't call yet," Serena tells her. "Not until we've seen them all up close."

I roll my eyes.

The market door slides open, and the trio emerges. The boys cross the street toward the parking lot.

They're heading back to their car.

Serena jumps up from her seat and starts pacing across the café's deck.

"Serena," I hiss. But she's already strutting down to the parking lot.

"Hey!" she calls to the boys.

They turn toward her. They seem to hesitate. They're suddenly wary.

"Are you guys partying tonight?"

The blond answers. "We could be."

Their voices are muffled now. Hollie and I are too far away to hear.

But I notice beach guy's gaze wander over me. He almost smiles, and then he looks away.

A minute later, Serena trots back to us, beaming. She waves her cell and whispers, "He gave me his number." She slips back into her seat. "Max." She says his name excitedly.

I look back at the lot as the boys reach their car.

"Adam." Max signals to my beach guy. "Throw me your keys, man. I want to drive."

Adam tosses his keys.

Max is driving now. The Dodge's engine revs, and the music starts up again.

I see Adam in the passenger's seat. As they tear onto the road, tires screeching on the hot tarmac, a shiver moves over me.

ADAM

That's my car. *That's my car.*

I want to shout it. I want to tell everyone to back away, because that's my car.

Someone took my keys.

Someone drove my car into the harbor.

My thoughts are spiraling, coming thick and fast.

Jenna is standing next to me. She hasn't moved in a while. I can't look at her.

That's my car.

She chokes out a cry.

Across the pavement, the police have approached something. They're crouching, leaning over a heap of blankets on the ground.

But they're not looking at the blankets. There's something under them. A person.

It's then that I notice there are officials from Rookwood here, too—Hank with his balding head and heavy trench, and Principal Lomax, dressed in jeans and a purple raincoat, like she's rushed straight over here from walking her dog. She probably has—because this is an emergency. They're standing together with their heads bowed, keeping a respectful distance as the cops inspect the body.

I can't hold back anymore. I sprint forward.

"Is it Tommy?" I hear my voice like a gunshot in the eerie quiet. My voice doesn't belong here. It's loud and frantic. This is a place for order and calm.

One of the cops grabs me. He holds me back, pinning my arms down, like he's afraid I might fight back.

Everything blurs. My car, the jetty, the cop. Jenna.

"Is it Tommy?"

Principal Lomax rushes to me. "Adam." She's saying my name. Asking me to stay calm. Asking me to breathe. Maybe I'm not breathing.

"Is it Tommy?" The questions limps out of my mouth again.

"No," she tells me. But I don't have time to think about what that means. Principal Lomax's lips are moving. The words are already out.

"It's Max."

Interview with Adam Cole,
conducted by Detective Drew Felton at 11:20 a.m.
on Saturday, October 13th.

D.F.: Adam. We meet again, it seems.

A.C.: Yeah.

D.F.: Adam, who might have had access to your car last night?

A.C.: I don't know. Any of the boys. They borrow my car all the time. I thought Max might have taken my keys.

D.F.: What made you think Max had taken your car?

A.C.: I was looking for my keys last night. I couldn't find them. I thought he took them.

D.F.: So, Max had your car keys?

A.C.: He must have, right? But I never thought he would do this. I never thought he'd kill himself.

D.F.: Let's circle back for a second, Adam, because I'm still not getting an answer from you. What made you think Max had taken your car keys last night?

A.C.: I thought he was going after someone. A girl.

D.F.: Why?

A.C.: He wanted to talk to her.

D.F.: About what?

A.C.: I don't know.

D.F.: Where were you last night, Adam?

A.C.: I was at Rookwood. Mostly.

D.F.: Mostly?

A.C.: I was at the pier for a minute. There was a vigil for Colleen O'Dell.

D.F.: Was Max with you?

A.C.: Yes.

D.F.: When was the last time you saw him?

A.C.: I don't know. Back at Rookwood. Early hours. I don't remember the exact time.

D.F.: Had you been drinking last night, Adam?

A.C.: No.

D.F.: Are you sure about that?

A.C.: Yes.

D.F.: Do you remember the last conversation you had with Max Grayson? Adam? Are you alright there, son? Adam...? Okay, I'm going to let you get some rest. We'll continue this again soon.

Interview terminated at 11:32.

BRIANNA: Serena, babe, we're all here for you. Please call.

IMOGEN: Please reply. Are you okay???

BRIANNA: Serena, we all love you and want to support you. Girls, maybe we should go over to her house?

IMOGEN: I'm already on my way. Jenna, are you coming?

SERENA: Please don't come over, Imogen. I just want to be alone.

JENNA

Outside of the group chat, I have a private message from Serena.

Come over. But just you, okay?

Even by the time I get to her house, I still have absolutely no idea what to say to her. When I woke up on Saturday morning, I thought I'd be breaking the news about Max cheating with Colleen. But now, a day later, I'm showing up to comfort her while she grieves over Max's sudden death.

A shadow approaches behind the frosted glass panel in the Blakes' front door. The door opens, and Serena's mom greets me with a weak smile.

"Hi, Mrs. Blake."

She blinks a couple of times, as if she's trying to place my face. I've met her before, but I've always felt like Mrs. Blake was kind of absent. Even when Serena and I were hanging out most days, I hardly ever saw her mom. Whenever we arrived at Serena's house, we were always greeted by the housekeeper. Serena's parents were usually out at some fancy function or party.

"I'm Jenna," I say, to jog her memory. "Serena's friend."

"Of course. Come in, Jenna." She smiles again, and for a second I'm struck by the family resemblance. She and Serena share the same glossy black hair and dark eyes. But more than that, there's a certain façade to the Blake women, something very poised and elegant even in the midst of chaos.

"How is she?" I ask as I step into the hallway.

Mrs. Blake sighs. "Well, she's struggling. This has devastated her, as you can imagine."

"Yes. I'm sure."

"Serena was besotted with that boy."

I dip my gaze. "I know. She really loved him."

She lets out another gentle breath. "It certainly seems that way. Did you know him well?"

The question catches me off guard. "No," I tell her. "Not really."

"He was quite something," she muses. "A lot of potential there. I must admit, I had my reservations about Serena getting involved with a boy from Rookwood."

I bristle at the comment.

"But Max," she carries on with a sigh, "he surprised me. He presented very well."

I muster a smile. Max, the master of deception.

"He was a big hit at the country club," she adds. "At first, I was sure Serena was only dating him to shock me or to get my attention, I don't know." She pauses and runs her fingers along her pearl necklace. "But now I see she was truly fond of him."

"She was devoted."

Mrs. Blake's gaze drifts to the wide staircase. "She's upstairs in her bedroom. You can go on up. You know the way?"

I nod. "Thanks."

"If you need anything…" She trails off, then lightly squeezes my arm before stepping aside.

Serena's bedroom is a world of mirrors and soft pinks, the bed piled high with throw cushions. She's sitting amongst the cushions with her knees tucked up to her chest. Her face is blotchy, and mascara is smudged beneath her watery eyes.

Her gaze lands on me, and fresh tears fill her eyes. "I just keep thinking," she whispers hoarsely, "this can't be real." A tear spills down her cheek, and she lets it fall.

I take a seat on the edge of her bed. "I'm so sorry. I wish there was something I could say or do to make this better."

She purses her lips, fighting back a sob. "Nothing can make this better, Jenna. He's gone." She gives way to a shattered breath. "Max is dead."

I drop my gaze, tracing the crisscross patterns on the bedding with my eyes. "I'm so sorry."

"This can't be real. It can't be."

"I know," I murmur.

Serena's phone pings, and she tosses it aside.

The new message flashes on top of a dozen other unread texts. "It's Imogen," I say, reading from her screen. "She just wants to make sure you're okay."

"She texted me a hundred times already. I can't deal with it right now."

"She's just worried about you. They all are."

"I said I can't deal, Jenna."

"Okay." I place my hand on her leg. "You don't have to."

"I loved him," she whispers.

"I know you did."

"We had plans. We had our future mapped out. We were going to start apartment shopping next week."

"Serena…"

"I loved him so much, Jenna." She rubs roughly at her eyes. "I thought I'd be married to him by this time next year."

"I'm sorry." My stomach tightens at the thought that Serena's memories would be forever tarnished if she found out what Max had been doing behind her back. Who he really was.

She swipes at a fresh tear. "Did you know he was in the passenger's seat? Did you know that?"

I look up, meeting the intensity of her stare. "What?"

"He was in the passenger's seat."

"Wait. Max wasn't driving?"

She shakes her head and sniffs. "He was in the passenger's seat. The cops told me. Someone else was driving. Someone *killed* him." She chokes out a ragged breath. "And the murdering asshole doesn't even have the balls to come forward and admit it."

A million thoughts race through my mind. Max wasn't driving. Someone *else* was behind the wheel of Adam's car. "But why didn't Max…?"

"Why didn't he get out of the car when it went over the jetty?" She wipes away another tear from her cheek. "They can't say until they get the toxicology report back, but the police think he may have been incapacitated."

"As in, high?"

"Yeah. That's what they're saying." She rolls her eyes.

"What, you don't buy it?"

"Max wasn't high. No way. He didn't do drugs, ever. He never wanted to lose control like that."

I grope for words. "Maybe it was just one time."

She grimaces. "No, Jenna. He'd drink, sure, but he was always in control. He got mad at me once for smoking pot."

"What are you saying? You think someone spiked his drink?"

She holds my gaze. "I was with him until about midnight that night. He was fine. He was going to go to bed after I left. And then, somehow, a few hours later, he's so off his head that he can't get out of a car that some shithead drove into the ocean?"

"Oh my god," I murmur. My heart starts beating double time.

"Who would do that to him? Who would be so *sick*?"

"I don't..."

"Who would hate him that much?"

Colleen.

I don't know why her smiling picture pops into my mind. Colleen is dead, and Max was her friend. But there's a chance that Max was the one who killed her.

Now Max is dead.

And it's looking like someone killed him.

"I need a ride tonight."

Colleen's voice rebounds across the locker room after gym class.

I look over at the vanity station, where Serena, Imogen, and

Brianna have been huddled for a while, immersed in applying their makeup. Colleen pushes herself forward, landing the prime spot in front of the mirror.

"Which one of you girls is driving tonight?"

There's a pause.

"Driving where?" Imogen asks.

Colleen rolls her eyes. "Where do you think? To Rookwood. Obviously. Same as every other Friday night."

"Were you invited?" Serena's voice is clipped.

"Of course I'm invited." Colleen matches her tone. "I'm there every week."

I watch them out of the corner of my eye as I lace up my sneakers. Serena's dark stare lingers on her own reflection in the mirror.

"Oh," she says, and her gaze travels over the reflections of Imogen and Brianna. There's something, a look, a tension between them and Colleen.

But Colleen doesn't seem to notice. Or care.

"So?" Colleen says. "Answer, please. Which one of you bitches is giving me a ride to Rookwood tonight?"

Serena pops the cap off her lip gloss and dabs on a layer. "Why can't you drive yourself?"

"Because I plan on getting annihilated, and I could do without a DUI."

"I can drive," Imogen says, and Serena jabs her in the ribs.

"Speaking of DUIs…" Colleen lowers her voice. "I heard the Rooks are getting some quality produce in tonight. Are you guys buying?"

The trio swap another look.

"Uh, no," Brianna says. "Colleen, you shouldn't be buying either. You don't even know where it's coming from. It could be anything."

Colleen snorts. "Okay, Mom. Maybe you should try something, Bri. It might loosen you up."

"I don't think so."

"Your loss."

"She's right, though, Colleen," Serena says. "It makes you look trashy and desperate. Like, you're all over the guys when you're wasted."

"Get a grip, Serena. I'm just having fun."

"You're making a fool of yourself, creeping around all the Rooks like a dog in heat."

Colleen smirks. "Oh. You poor thing."

Serena turns to face her. "What?"

"I'm not interested in your boyfriend, if that's what you're getting at. I don't do leftovers. We're friends, that's all."

Serena gives a tight laugh. "He's not interested in you either, Colleen. Not even as a friend."

"Okay." She flips her hair and turns on her heel. "Whatever, jealous," she calls as she struts out of the locker room. "Pick me up at eight, Imogen."

The door thuds shut behind her.

I see Serena's jaw clench in the mirror. When she notices my gaze on her reflection, she forces a smile.

I muster one back.

ADAM

I walk around aimlessly in the darkness, just pacing through the forest, because I don't know what else to do. I don't know where else to go.

Max is gone. And it's my fault. I should never have told Jenna about him cheating. I screwed him over. That's probably why he drove my car off the jetty.

If it gets back to the cops about him and Colleen, that's motive. That's his ass on the line. Anyway, without Serena, his plans for the future were screwed too. And it's my fault.

I lean against a tree and close my eyes, pressing my palms against the rough bark.

Max took my car. He wanted to send me one last message. One last "fuck you."

Because I killed him.

That's what happens to people who get close to me. Sooner or later, they're going to wind up dead.

JENNA: Meet me?

ADAM: I can't.

JENNA: Please. We need to talk.

JENNA: Adam?

ADAM: I'll be there.

JENNA

It's dark out. I follow the path of lanterns down to the craggy beach. Adam is already there, sitting on the rocks. He's toying with a pebble, tossing it into the air and catching it in his palm. Even in the darkness I can see how restless he is. How uneasy he is.

His gaze stays trained on the water as I sit down beside him. I brush the sand off my hands. "Thanks for coming. Sorry, I know it's late."

"It's alright. I was awake." His voice is low and quiet, nearly swallowed by the sound of the surging waves.

I hesitate, focused on the tide. "Why didn't you want to meet?"

"I wanted to." His eyes are lost on the black ocean. "But I shouldn't. *You* shouldn't. You shouldn't be around me. I'm no good for you." He throws the pebble, and I hear it clink in the darkness.

"Adam, I have to talk to you about something. There's no easy way to say this."

He turns to face me.

"I was just at Serena's house," I explain.

"Yeah? How is she?"

"Not good." I shiver. It's colder today, the night air is damp and tastes salty as it rushes around us. "Serena told me something that I feel like you should know too. Max wasn't driving your car."

There's a beat of silence.

He shakes his head, confused. "What?"

"Max wasn't driving. Someone else was."

Frown lines crease his brow. "What do you mean? Who was driving?"

"I don't know, but Max was in the passenger seat when the car went into the water."

He stills, and his lips part. "No. Max was driving. He killed himself."

I touch his shoulder. "Max didn't do this," I murmur.

"I don't..." He drags his hands over his face. "Are you sure Serena's got this right?"

"She seems pretty convinced." I exhale into the night. "I'm sure this will all be made public, anyway. Once the press finds out."

He stares back at me, silently.

"I wanted to tell you before you heard it from anyone else," I say. "I thought you should know."

"You're sure he wasn't driving?"

There's nothing more I can say.

He lets out a shattered sound and scrubs his hands through his hair. "So, who was?"

I don't answer. I don't know how to.

"You think she did it?"

For a second, I wonder if he means Colleen, just like my mind had jumped to her when I was faced with the same question. But then I remember. "No," I tell him, softly. "I don't think Serena did it."

"Did you tell her? About Max cheating on her?"

I shake my head. "No."

"That night, the night Max died, you said you were going to tell her."

"I know. But I didn't. I still haven't."

"The last time I saw him..." He pauses, lost in his own words. "The last time I saw him, I came clean to him about what I told you. About him cheating. That was the last conversation I had with him." A few long seconds pass before he speaks again. "How are you so sure that Serena doesn't know about Max cheating?"

"Because I know Serena."

"You *think* you know her."

"She was home by midnight," I relay to him. "Her mom has given an alibi that she heard Serena come in around that time and she didn't leave again after. What happened to Max happened way after she left the cabin."

"You're sure?" he presses.

"Yes. I know you don't want to hear it, but it's true. Serena was at home when this happened."

"And she couldn't have come back?"

"She was home. The alarm system in her house has all the times logged."

I fall quiet, listening to the hiss of the surf as the gale drives the breakers into the shore.

Adam's gaze becomes distant, lost on the moonlit ocean again. "The cops questioned me. They would have known that Max wasn't in the driver's seat. They didn't tell me." He laughs under his breath. "They must think it's me. They must think I was driving."

"You can't jump to conclusions like that. You don't know what they're thinking."

"It was my car."

"Well," I say, and blow out a breath, "plenty of people would have seen you at the cabin or in the dorms. You'll have an alibi."

He catches my gaze. "I wasn't at Rookwood on Friday night. Not the whole time."

I stare back at him for a long moment. "Where were you?"

There's another pause before he answers. "Your house."

"What?"

"After I told Max about you knowing that he'd been cheating, he took off. I couldn't find him. And I couldn't find my car keys." He grimaces as he relives the memory, and my pulse starts to quicken. "I started thinking maybe he'd gone looking for you, so I went to your house. I wanted to make sure that Max hadn't tracked you down."

I scramble for words. "How do you even know where I live?" The surreal memory of someone standing on my lamplit street flashes through my mind.

Adam.

"We talked about it. You told me. Way back when we first met." His eyes skate over the dark shore. "Maybe you don't remember it, but—"

"I do remember." My voice is quiet.

"After what happened to Colleen, I couldn't... I would never have forgiven myself if I didn't..." The words fall away from his lips, and he winces. He offers me a wry smile. "Do you think I'm a creep for showing up at your house?"

I gaze down at my hands. "No."

"I just didn't want to take any chances. Turns out, I was following the wrong person. Or at least for the wrong reasons, anyway. I should have been watching out for Max." He pauses and rubs his hands over his face. "The last time I spoke to him, it didn't end well."

I draw in a slow breath.

He picks up another stone and tosses it into the night, way more forcefully this time. "I won't get a chance to make things right with Max."

"I'm sorry," I whisper. And in that moment, sitting beside Adam, here, on our beach and seeing the pain in his gaze, I feel the urgency of life, as though any minute he could disappear. All of this could disappear. I could disappear.

"I'm sorry too," he replies, his eyes shifting back to the waves crashing in front of us. "I never wanted to lie to you. I don't know if you can believe that, but I swear it's true. From the moment I met you..." The sentence trails off.

"What?" I ask softly.

He musses his hair. "I don't know. From the moment I met you, I knew I needed to know you. Your perspective, your intuition. You make me feel like I'm more than what I am."

And suddenly I know what I've been hiding from myself, what I've been pushing aside amidst all of this chaos.

I want him, and I can't pretend that I don't. Not in this moment, when it's just the two of us, with nothing but the rush of the ocean and the tick of time passing us by.

Before I even know what I'm doing, I lean in to him and

my lips brush his. I pull him closer to me, feeling his cool lips on mine, tasting the salt air between us. His breathing quickens.

It's just the two of us—the rest of the world has melted away. My hands are on his arms, and then the nape of his neck. I feel his heart beating fast against mine, his breath on my lips.

I pull him closer, and the darkness covers us.

ADAM

For the first time in a really long while, I feel like I have something to lose.

It's dawn by the time I get back to Rookwood. Tommy is comatose in his bed, breathing steadily beneath the covers. I let the dorm door slam shut, waking him.

"Where the hell have you been all weekend?"

He blinks back at me in the dull light. "What?"

"Where were you all weekend? I've been going out of my mind."

"Does it matter where I was? I'm back now." His voice is bleary, thick with sleep.

"You weren't answering my calls."

"My cell died."

It's a lie. I know it is. But I don't challenge him.

He stares at me, strangely. "What's up with you?" he asks.

"Max was in the passenger seat of my car."

Tommy sits up and rubs his eyes with the heels of his

hands. His hair is wild and falling over his brow. "What are you talking about?"

"Max. He was in the passenger seat of my car."

His face is blank.

"Someone drove my car off the jetty," I tell him. "You haven't heard?"

"Shit." He yawns into the heel of his hand. "Is it a write-off?"

My car. He thinks this is about my car.

"Max…" I swallow hard. "Max drowned. He's dead."

Suddenly, Tommy is alert, sober. "What? What do you mean?"

I stand near his bed, tense. "Max is dead."

"No." He shakes his head, then rakes his hands roughly through his hair. "No way. He can't be. He isn't."

I search his eyes. My next words jump from nowhere, rushing to the surface before I can pull them back. "Did you do it? Were you driving?"

His jaw drops. "What?"

I suck in my lip. "Were you the one behind the wheel?"

He starts to laugh. It's a hollow sound. "I can't believe you're saying this to me right now. A minute ago I was asleep, Adam. You wake me up, tell me my buddy's dead, and then, what? Accuse me of killing him?"

"Someone took my car."

"You're losing it, man—"

"Alright." My throat burns and my voice is shaking. "But you disappeared. You've been MIA all weekend. Your phone's been off—"

He shrinks back from me. "So? That doesn't mean I *killed* Max. Why would you even think that?"

I take a breath, trying to steady myself. "I'm sorry. I don't really think that. I'm just…" I trail my knuckles over my mouth. "Max was hiding something, and now he's dead. And we still don't know anything. First Colleen and now Max… On top of all of that, you've been avoiding me all weekend. I needed your help, and you weren't here."

"Okay. I—"

"Why weren't you answering my calls, Tommy?"

He doesn't speak. He just stares down at his hands.

"Because I saw you with that guy?"

He sucks in a rough breath. His neck flushes red.

I cross the room and take a seat on my bed, facing him. "Tommy." I try to catch his wandering gaze. "You can talk to me. If you want. I'm not going to judge you or treat you any differently."

He won't meet my eyes.

"You don't have to hide who you are," I tell him. "Not from me."

There's a silence between us, as the wind outside rattles the windowpane.

When he finally speaks, he sounds tired. "I wondered if you knew. Before."

I nod but say nothing.

He gnaws on his lower lip. "His name's Chris."

"Maybe you'll introduce us sometime."

We fall quiet again.

"Are you okay?" I ask him.

His jaw clenches as he swallows. "Max's dead."

I stare down at the floorboards, breathing slowly.

"Is this real?" Tommy murmurs.

My heart aches at the question. "I wish it wasn't."

Tommy bows his head. After a moment, he speaks again. "You ever worry about the future, Adam?"

On reflex, my hands ball. "Yeah."

"You ever get scared about what'll happen to us after Rookwood?" He threads his fingers together and stares down at his hands.

I remember Max's words last summer, back when he first met Serena. She was his meal ticket after we graduated. With her, he'd never have to go back to where he came from. "We'll figure it out, Tommy. We'll look out for each other."

"You think you'll go home?"

I shake my head.

"I don't want to go back, either," he says.

"You won't have to. You're outta there."

"I'm scared I'll never truly be out."

They're probably the most honest words I've ever heard him say.

"You're wrong, Tommy. You've already gotten out. You're only dealing because you're sending your dad the money, right? You're still working for the guy?"

He won't say it, but he doesn't have to. I know.

"You can stop. You're done. It isn't you, Tommy. Don't screw up your life, not when you're so close to breaking free. We're at Rookwood so that we can turn our lives around. You said it yourself, this is our second chance."

"We shouldn't be talking about this right now. Max—"

"Cops are going to be crawling all over the place. They

already are. They're going to be asking questions. Get rid of the drugs."

"I will," he says.

"And get your alibi straight."

He looks at me. I see something in his expression. He's afraid. I am, too.

"I didn't kill Max," he says at last.

"I know. I'm sorry. I'm just... Someone did this on our own turf. Someone was close enough to take my keys. Someone was close enough to get Max into my car. Max is dead, and we've all got blood on our hands."

I stand and pace around the room as scattered pictures spill through my mind. My car, the harbor, the EMTs.

Max.

Colleen.

The memories haunt me.

"What about you?" Tommy's voice pulls me back. "It was your car. Have you got an alibi?"

I remember the feel of the pavement beneath my sneakers while I stood outside Jenna's house, my heart hammering as I waited for Max to show up. But he never showed. "No. I was alone."

"I'll cover for you. If the cops ask, we were together."

And just like that, the lying starts again.

GARDINERS BAY DAILY PRESS

Monday, October 15th
Article written by Jorge Hernandez.

Emergency Services were called to Gardiners Bay harbor in the early hours of Saturday morning to reports of a car submerged in the water.

The driver is yet to be identified and was missing from the scene. A young male was recovered from the front passenger's side of the submerged vehicle. The male was pronounced dead at the scene, and the family has been informed. He has been identified as eighteen-year-old Max Grayson.

Searches continue for the driver, who is presumed to have survived the accident.

A local resident has commented, "I heard a crashing sound in the early hours, so I looked out my window. Someone ran across the harbor, but it was too dark to make out any details. I thought it was just kids fooling around. The Rookwood boys go down there sometimes."

This is Gardiners Bay's second young life lost tragically in a matter of weeks, following the death of seventeen-year-old Colleen O'Dell last month. Questions continue to surround a possible connection between the two incidents.

Gardiners Bay Police Department have declined to comment at this time.

JENNA

I wake to the sound of my phone ringing. Daylight is streaming through my window, but I couldn't have been asleep for long. I came home just as the sun was rising, creeping into the house like a thief, holding my breath in fear that at any moment, a wrong step could wake Kate. She'd flip if she knew I'd stayed out all night. On Rookwood Beach. With Adam.

I can still feel his touch on my skin. The memory makes me shiver. I don't want it to go away.

Still half-asleep, I fumble as I reach for my phone. *Hollie* lights up the screen, with a backdrop of a picture of the two of us together last summer, grinning at the camera. A snapshot in time before any of this happened.

I press answer. "Hol?" My voice sounds bleary.

"Hey. I didn't wake you, did I?"

Outside, the sun has risen, but it's still a little earlier than my alarm is set.

I sit upright and comb my fingers through the tangles in

my hair. Grains of sand fall free from the knots. "No. Is everything okay?"

"I'm okay. Sorry I didn't call you back over the weekend. There's just been so much going on. I had my meeting with the police on Saturday."

I hold the phone close to my ear. "How did it go?"

"They didn't arrest me. They only wanted to talk to me about transitioning back to school."

I exhale in relief. "That's good, right?"

"Yeah! My lawyer seems to think that anything they had against me was all circumstantial and the detectives are looking elsewhere."

"But didn't you say more evidence had come to light?"

"Apparently they're looking into the finger marks or something, but there was no direct connection to me. Nothing that could lead to my arrest."

I press my hand to my heart. "Hol, I'm so happy for you."

"I'm happy for me, too!" She laughs, and for the first time in a really long while, she sounds like Hollie again. "Finally, we can start to put this in the past."

"What about school? Are you coming back?"

"Yes. Today."

"That's great."

"I'm freaking out, though." She lets out a nervous breath. "Does everyone still hate me?"

"No. Of course not."

"How's Serena?" she asks quickly. "I heard about Max. Is she doing okay?"

I chew on my thumbnail. "Not really. I saw her yesterday.

She's sad. She's angry. What can you say to someone who's just lost their boyfriend?"

"I've been meaning to call her. Maybe I should. But with everything that's been going on lately…"

"Serena understands."

"It seems like people are thinking that Colleen's and Max's deaths are related incidents. I guess you were right to be suspicious of the Rooks. It was probably one of them."

A chill moves over me. I hug my duvet closer to my chest.

"I really should call Serena." Hollie's voice goes quiet. "We've just drifted apart."

"She knows you care about her. She cares about you, too."

"Yeah," she sighs. "Maybe." She hesitates for a moment. "Will you meet me before class? I'm having major anxiety about walking into school alone."

"Of course I'll meet you. Where?"

"Parking lot," she says. "An hour?"

"You got it."

We end the call, and I drag myself to the bathroom. I stand under the shower and watch the few grains of sand that are still clinging to my skin fall away and disappear into the drain.

By the time I reach the wrought iron gates of Preston, Hollie's car is parked beneath a willow tree. She's still in the driver's seat. Her sunglasses are covering most of her face as she stares through the windshield. Clusters of girls wearing the Preston plaid-skirt and white-shirt combo are shooting the odd glance at her cherry-red VW Bug as they stroll past.

I slip into the passenger seat and close the door behind me. Hollie swivels to face me. She pushes her sunglasses onto her head, trapping stray wisps of blond hair. "I shouldn't be here. This is a huge mistake."

"You'll be fine. You had to come back, eventually. It may as well be now."

A group of juniors walks past. Their eyes skate over us through the windshield.

I notch up my smile for Hollie's benefit. "It'll be fine. By lunch, you'll be yesterday's news."

I swing open my door, and Hollie follows my lead. Side by side, we cross the manicured lawn and brick walkways, and fall in sync with the other girls heading into the building.

Nobody really says anything. A few people shoot wary looks our way or smile awkwardly at us. I link my arm through Hollie's as we brave the arched hallways toward homeroom.

"You've got this," I whisper to Hollie. "You have nothing to hide. You've done nothing wrong."

She nods.

We've got this.

But I stop short when we cross into the classroom.

Serena is in her usual seat at the back of the room.

I catch her gaze. "You're here?" I mouth. I hadn't expected her to show up to class today. It's been less than forty-eight hours since the news of Max's death broke. It was only yesterday that I held her hand while she sobbed into her pillow.

She shrugs back at me. Her dark eyes are still puffy from crying, but now her watery gaze is replaced by a blank and tired stare.

Brianna and Imogen are seated at their desks on either side of her. Their eyes linger on Hollie and me.

Mrs. Gordon steps into class with the clickety-clack of

high heels, and I catch Serena's glazed gaze once more. "Talk later," I mouth, and she nods.

At lunch, Hollie and I take our trays to the picnic tables outside. The cafeteria is claustrophobic at the best of times, and with Hollie under the social microscope, the last place we need to be is in the lunchroom.

I set my tray down and slide into the seat opposite Hollie. "So, how bad has it been on a scale of one to ten?"

She raises an eyebrow. "One being the best, ten being the worst?"

I nod.

"Um…" She ponders over the question for a second. "About an eight."

"Eight? That's not bad. It's two better than a full ten."

"True," she says, prodding at her potato salad. "It's been okay, I guess. People are whispering, though. I know they are."

I roll my eyes. "When are they *not* whispering?"

"Valid point. It's been better than I expected, actually. Nobody's even mentioned Colleen yet, so that's good."

"See, I told you. You're already old news."

She feigns insult. "Excuse you."

"I meant that in the best possible way."

I still haven't told Hollie about Max's fling with Colleen. I want to tell her. I *should* tell her. But the words won't seem to come out. Maybe because I know that once I say it, once I put the information out there, I can't take it back.

"Jenna!"

I glance over my shoulder just as Imogen is crossing the

quad. Her blond hair is glistening in the low sunlight, and her cheer skirt is fluttering in the breeze as she paces toward us.

She comes to a stop at our table. "Jenna, can I speak with you?"

Hollie and I exchange a glance.

"Sure. Is everything okay?"

"Yeah. I just wanted to talk to you. About Serena." Her eyes wander over Hollie. "Alone, if you don't mind."

I shoot Hollie a quick look, and she nods. "I'll be right back," I tell her.

Imogen sets off across the quad, and I follow her to a quiet spot beneath the willow trees.

"What's going on?"

She's gnawing at her perfectly glossed lips. "Serena. You know she ditched right after homeroom?"

"I'm surprised she came to school at all."

Imogen takes a shaky breath. "I'm really worried about her, Jenna. She totally flipped out at Bri, over nothing. She won't talk to us about how she's feeling, and Bri doesn't even seem to care."

"Well, it'll take time, I guess. When Serena's ready to talk, she will."

"I hope so," she says in a soft voice. "I'm just so worried about her. Has she talked to you at all?"

I hold up my hands, helplessly. "A little."

"Jenna…" She hesitates, biting her lip again. "There is something Serena told me. Something bad."

A breeze stirs the branches above us, and my stomach knots. "Bad, like how?"

Imogen starts fiddling with her necklace. "Has she told you about the thing with Max?"

"What do you mean?"

"About Max, and…" She lowers her voice. "About what happened."

I search her eyes, trying to unpick her comment. And then it dawns on me.

My heart starts beating fast. She knows. Imogen knows about Max and Colleen. Which means Serena knows about Max and Colleen, too.

I grope for words.

Imogen wraps her arms around herself. "Do you know about what happened?"

I glance over my shoulder. There are people passing us on the quad, but everyone seems too absorbed in their own conversations to pay any attention to us. I keep my voice hushed. "About the cheating?"

She draws in a sharp breath.

And I wince. *Oh, no.*

"What cheating?"

Stupid, stupid, stupid!

Her words start coming out fast. "Tell me, Jenna. You have to tell me. Was Max cheating on Serena? Who with?"

"I don't know!"

She presses her hands to her face.

"What did *you* mean?" I ask quickly. "What did *you* know about Max?"

"That he wasn't driving the car," she splutters. "Not that he was…" She lowers her voice. "Cheating."

"Listen, Imogen, you can't tell anyone. Serena can't find out about this now. It'll destroy her."

She stares back at me in disbelief. "How do you even know this, anyway? Who told you?"

"That's not important—"

"Was it Max? Did Max tell you?"

"No. It was Adam."

The moment I say his name, Imogen's shoulders relax, and she half laughs.

I blink in confusion. "What's so funny?"

"Jenna, word of advice. You can't trust Adam Cole. Don't believe anything he tells you, okay?"

All of a sudden, my skin feels hot. "What makes you say that?"

"Everyone knows! The guy's a pathological liar. It's like the thing he's known for. Plus, he's dangerous! Haven't you heard what he did?"

A bolt of fear shoots through me. "What he did?" I echo, numbly.

She pauses while a group of freshmen girls pass us with their lunch trays. "Yeah," she says under her breath. "Jenna, he killed his mom."

GOOGLE SEARCH: Adam Cole

Adam Cole Profiles | LinkedIn
View the profiles of professionals named Adam Cole...

Find Friends on Facebook | Adam Cole
100+ people named Adam Cole. Find Friends on Facebook...

Real Estate Agent Adam Ben Cole
Contact Adam Ben Cole, one of the few agents whose property...

HOLLIE: Hey, lady. What are you up to? I have a free period!

JENNA: I'm in Study Hall. Just internet searching. Stopping now.

HOLLIE: Oh, yeah? What are you searching for?

JENNA: Nothing. I'm being stupid.

HOLLIE: ???

JENNA: Honestly, nothing. Imogen said something earlier that weirded me out for a second, but I'm over it now. So, free period, huh? Wanna meet at the library?

ADAM

Classes carry on as normal on Monday. Nothing has changed. Well, something has changed. Max is gone.

And *we're* different today. The mood has shifted. Everyone's quiet, subdued. Even Scotch.

The sun streams through the window, contrasting the darkness inside the classroom. I keep my head down, staring at the words on my paper, at the curve of my own handwriting. I don't think I'll remember a single line of what I've written.

I think about Max.

I think about Tommy.

I think about Jenna.

It's right after lunch when the cops show up. I'm not dumb, I know they're here for me. When Rookwood's secretary, Miss Morgan, knocks on the classroom door and discreetly hands Ms. Omar a slip of paper, I wait, watch, until both sets of eyes flicker to me.

"Adam." Ms. Omar says my name. She beckons me to the front of the room.

The class is silent now. I'm talking pin-drop silent. In all my days at Rookwood, I've never heard the wall clock tick before. My chair scrapes. I walk across the room.

The cops, I think. Just say it. Everyone already knows. It was my car. Max drowned in the passenger's seat of my crappy old Dodge.

I follow Miss Morgan along the corridor, and our footsteps echo off the high ceiling. Miss Morgan has always been nice enough. She's the type of person that smiles a lot, kind of young. Young compared to the rest of the staff here, anyway. At a guess, I'd say she's midtwenties, with neat blond hair and rosy cheeks. She wears older clothes, though—these woolen calf-length skirts and white ruffled shirts.

She directs me to a seat in the reception waiting area. There's a small partition window looking into the principal's office. People are already in the room: the two cops are sitting across from Principal Lomax. My palms start to sweat. I rub my hands on the coarse green fabric of the waiting room sofa.

"You want a glass of water, Adam?" Miss Morgan's voice makes my head snap up. She's hovering at the water cooler, holding a disposable cup that she's already popped from the dispenser.

"Yeah," I say. "Thanks."

The cooler hums and clicks while she fills the cup. Then she comes over and hands it to me. It's hard to swallow, but I do it, just so I have something to do.

Through the partition window, I see Principal Lomax stand. A moment later, her office door opens. "Adam." She smiles warmly at me. "We're ready for you now."

I knock back the water and crumple the plastic cup before

tossing it into the wastepaper basket. Then, just like that, I'm in the office, sitting with the two cops, listening to the buzz of the air conditioner. Principal Lomax has pulled her chair back, giving us some space without actually leaving the room.

"Adam Cole." The man jumps right into it. "I'm Detective Drew Felton. We've met before." He's balding, in his midfifties, easy. This isn't his first rodeo. "And this is my colleague, Detective Kate Dallas." Jenna's aunt offers me a thin smile. "We're just here to ask you a couple more questions about your friend Max Grayson."

"Alright." I rub the back of my neck. "But don't I need a lawyer present for this?"

Felton's dark eyes bore into me. "This is just an informal chat, son."

"Just a couple of questions," Dallas echoes.

"Your principal is welcome to sit in if that would make you more comfortable," Felton continues. "You are still a minor, after all."

Principal Lomax speaks up. "Adam, if it's okay with you, I'm going to stay right here during the interview."

"Yeah." I scratch at the clammy skin on my palms as I glance across the office. Principal Lomax's chair is pulled so far into the corner that she's nearly touching the hydrangea. But she's here.

That's good. I need someone right now. Someone I trust.

"Yeah, no problem," I say.

Jenna's aunt speaks again. "As Detective Felton said, I'm Detective Kate Dallas."

I stare evenly back at her.

She clears her throat. "Am I right in saying that you and

Max Grayson were close friends?" She's holding a little note-pad, ready to jot down every bombshell I drop.

"Yeah, we were."

"And, to confirm, it was your car, a 1998 Dodge Aries, that Max's body was recovered from on Saturday?"

Her words are cold and flat. Principal Lomax shoots me a sympathetic look, but I get it. I know the drill. This isn't my first rodeo, either.

"Yeah, it was my car."

Dallas leans back in her seat. "Tell us, Adam, who else would have—or could have—had access to your motor ve-hicle during the early hours of Saturday morning?"

"Pretty much anyone." It only takes a second to weigh up my options. If I tell them about the parties we've been hav-ing at the cabin, it'll all be over, for everyone.

I'm glad.

Nothing good came of that damn cabin anyway. I want it gone.

"We were having a party," I say, "in the forest. I left my keys in the abandoned hunting cabin. Anyone who was at the party could have taken them."

In the corner, Principal Lomax cringes. I can practically feel the shame emitting from her. This wouldn't reflect well on her, or the initiative of the school. Parties taking place on a lockdown campus? Not good.

The cops look between each other.

"We've spoken to a lot of Max's friends," Felton responds. He's eyeballing me. "No one has mentioned a party."

I arch an eyebrow. "No kidding? I bet if it was their asses on the chopping block they'd be singing like canaries too."

Dallas leans forward. "Can you tell us the names of all the people who attended this party?" There's a lilt to her voice. *Alleged* party is what she wants to say. She probably thinks I'll claim just about anything at this point, if it means I've got a shot at saving myself.

"No," I tell her. "I can't do that."

Felton gives a lazy smirk. "Son, you need to start talking."

I'm not your son. That's my default response. But I keep my mouth shut.

Dallas's focus moves to Principal Lomax. "How are parties taking place at this school? Where is the security to prevent this?"

Principal Lomax struggles for words. "I can assure you, detectives, that our night security guard knows nothing about this, and we will put immediate strategies in place to stop this from—"

"It's not her fault," I interrupt. "It's not the school's fault. We're pretty good at covering our tracks."

Their attention is back on me.

"So, tell us, Adam," Felton carries on. "What was going on at this party? Were kids drinking alcohol? Taking drugs?"

"I don't know."

"But you were there?"

"For some of it, yeah."

He rubs his jaw. "And you say you left your keys there?"

"Yes."

He doesn't buy it. Neither of them does.

Felton is losing patience with me. His moustache twitches. "A boy died on Saturday. Do you understand the severity of this?"

"Yes, sir, I do. He was my best friend." My chest tightens as I say the words. I clench my teeth.

"Then cooperate. This is a murder investigation, and right now you're looking like a suspect."

Principal Lomax stands abruptly. "I think that's enough. Any further questions will require a lawyer to be present."

I stand, too. "I didn't kill Max." My words bounce off the walls. "I know you think I did. I know how it looks with my car and all, but I didn't do it. And I don't know who did, either."

The two detectives watch me. I can read their expressions, and they're right.

Even if I did know who killed Max, there's not a chance in hell I'd tell them.

ADAM: Cops came to the school today. Your aunt and the other guy. They questioned me about Max.

JENNA: And...?

ADAM: Meet?

JENNA

I texted Kate on my way to Rookwood Beach and told her I'd be home late. I lied and said I was working on a science project at school. I never used to lie to Kate. Now, it's become such a habit that I almost don't realize I'm doing it.

Don't be too late, she writes back. We need to talk.

Great.

When I arrive at the beach, Adam is walking across the rocks from the opposite direction.

I pull him into a hug as soon as I reach him. His lips brush against mine, and a shiver moves over me. A good shiver. The kind that makes my heart skip a beat.

Whatever rumors have been spread about him, they're wrong. I know they're wrong.

We sit on the shoreline, watching the tide drag in and out. I lean against his shoulder, my fingers entwined with his.

The sun has slipped behind a bank of rain clouds, looming gray overhead.

Adam runs his knuckles along the damp pebbles. "The cops think I killed Max."

I look up and study his profile.

"Because it was my car," he adds. "They think I did it."

"What did you tell them?"

"That there was a party and anyone could have taken my keys."

I trail my thumb along his palm. "Well, it's true."

"Yeah. That's what I told them."

"Did they accept it?"

He shrugs. "No. Probably not. But I haven't been arrested yet."

I stare at the horizon. It's fuzzy out there, as though the rain has already started far off in the distance.

"The school called my dad." Adam's voice gets lost somewhere, tangled in the breeze. "It must be serious if they're getting him involved."

"Why is that a bad thing?"

He sighs deeply. "My dad doesn't need to be part of this. He'll probably think I did it." The sentence is punctuated with a desolate laugh.

"He's your dad. He won't think that. Maybe he can help."

"Not much chance of that. You don't know my dad. The guy doesn't exactly have a high opinion of me." He catches my gaze and smiles ruefully.

"What do you mean?"

When he doesn't respond, I think back to Imogen's words from earlier today. About Adam's mom. It was just a senseless rumor. A stupid, senseless rumor that I shouldn't even be giving a second thought to.

"What happened between you and your dad?"

All of a sudden, his eyes are hard. "We don't get along. He skipped out on my mom and me when I was a kid. I don't see the guy anymore."

"What about your mom?" The question slips from my lips too fast.

His whole body seems to tense in response.

I sit up straighter. "You don't have to tell me anything if—"

"They think I killed my mother," he mutters into the breeze.

I grope for a reply. It's one thing hearing a rumor from Imogen, certified gossip, but to hear him say these words, like he's not even shocked by them? He carries on before I have a chance to string together a response.

"I didn't kill my mom."

I shake my head. "Of course. I never believed it—"

"Someone told you?"

I take a shaky breath.

"Was it Colleen? Did Colleen tell you I did?"

My stomach flips at the mention of her name. "What do you mean? How is Colleen involved in this?"

"After she lost it with Max," he says. "The night she disappeared. She threatened to tell people that I killed my mother. She wanted to hit me hard, I figure."

"Wait…" I blink back at him, trying to organize my racing thoughts. "Colleen threatened *you* on the night she was murdered? I thought she threatened Max?"

"Yeah. Me, Max, and Tommy. She went up against all of us."

A knot of fear builds inside my chest. Suddenly, I remember seeing marks on his arm right after we found Colleen. Scratch marks. Like fingernails.

My hand slips from his, and I squeeze my eyes shut. It was *his* car. Someone drove *his* car into the harbor, with Max in the passenger seat.

Colleen threatened Adam...

He went after Max too.

"Are you okay?" His fingers graze mine.

I shrink away.

He pulls his hand back, too. "Sorry. I didn't mean to..." He trails off.

I jump to my feet. "No. I'm sorry." I trip over my words. "I just remembered... I have to..." I don't finish the sentence.

He lowers his gaze and nods.

I don't look back as I stumble across the beach.

Focusing my attention on some mindless TV show seemed like a good idea an hour ago. It seemed like the perfect way to distract myself from the grim thoughts churning on a loop in my brain. But it doesn't work. I just stare at the screen, hugging a cushion to my chest as I watch some impossibly pretty girl tell an impossibly pretty guy that she's into him. I try not to think about Adam. And I kid myself that it's working.

"Jenna, we need to talk."

Kate's voice startles me. She paces into the living room. Judging by the tension in her expression, whatever she's about to talk to me about isn't good.

"That boy you were with on Friday night, after Colleen O'Dell's vigil."

I pause the TV and try to find my voice. "Adam?"

"Yes. Adam. I take it you've been spending quite a bit of time with the boys from Rookwood?" She arches an eyebrow—a disapproving eyebrow.

My throat feels dry all of a sudden. "Not all of them. Just him."

"Have you heard anything about parties taking place on Rookwood's campus?"

I stare down at the TV remote in my hands because I can't bring myself to look at Kate. "Yes. There are parties."

"Right." Her voice is tense. "And do you go to these parties?"

"No," I say, quickly. My cheeks start to feel hot. "I've been to some, but not lately."

"I see." She folds her arms.

"I'm sorry."

"Two kids have died in a matter of weeks," Kate mutters. "And they're both connected to that damn school. The last thing I need right now is for you to get caught up in that, Jenna."

"I know." I poke absently at the buttons on the remote. "I shouldn't have gone. Believe me, I won't be going again."

"You're damn right you shouldn't have gone."

"I should have told you," I add.

"Yes. You should have."

I force myself to meet her eyes. "Kate?"

She stares back at me, waiting.

"They're connected, aren't they? Max and Colleen, their deaths are connected."

She doesn't reply.

"Who do you think did it?"

She sighs and runs her fingers across her brow. "I don't have the answer to that yet."

"Who do you think?" I press.

"Two kids died," she says. "They knew each other, and, by the looks of things, they spent a lot of time together. Someone, for whatever reason, wanted them gone. When we find a motive, we find the person."

"So, that's it? You just need to find the motive that connects them?"

She lowers her gaze. "That about sums it up."

At least that answers one question: the detectives are still looking into possible motives beyond Hollie's argument with Colleen. Well, I know motives. I know a few. Serena's, Adam's—they're connected to both Colleen and Max.

I should be telling Kate this. I should have told her days ago.

But something still doesn't feel right.

As much as I want to come clean to Kate, and I owe her that respect, I can't bring myself to say their names.

Not yet.

There's something I'm missing. I know it.

ADAM

I stare at my reflection in the grimy mirror.

Sometimes, I feel like I don't know myself. The person in the mirror is just this shell, this skin that I walk around in. It's like I'm living in some screwed-up matrix, where the guy in the mirror isn't who I think he is. He can't be trusted.

Max. Tommy. Jenna. Sooner or later, they all lose trust in me.

Just like my dad did.

I don't know how things got so bad between me and him. He's not like Tommy's dad. He never was. But he closed the door on me, that's for sure. Maybe I'm just a painful memory for him, a reminder of his broken past. A reminder of a life he'd rather erase.

Or maybe it's more than that. It's crossed my mind plenty of times over the years, during those long nights staring up into the darkness. Maybe he thinks I killed her. Maybe he thinks I'm too far gone to save.

Maybe I think that, too.

I saw the look in Jenna's eyes when I told her about Colleen threatening me. I saw the fear.

She thinks I killed Colleen. She thinks I killed Max too. Because who else had more motive than me? Maybe I got into a fight with Max that night, and I lost it with him. I'd buy that.

My reflection stares back at me.

I want to call Jenna. I want to beg her to hear me out. Beg her to come back and forgive me for the things I didn't do. I want her to look at me the way she did before, because I care about her. I let myself care about her.

But I won't call her.

Just like I don't call my dad.

I don't want them to see that I'm hurting. I'm too proud for that.

I figure that's how I ended up at Rookwood.

IMOGEN: Has anyone heard from Serena?

BRIANNA: She hasn't responded to my texts.

IMOGEN: Should we go to her house?

BRIANNA: No way. She's being such a bitch. I can't.

IMOGEN: Bri. Come on. She's just lost her boyfriend.

BRIANNA: Wait. She's just replied to my DM. She says she doesn't want to talk to anyone. See? Bitch.

JENNA

It takes me a moment to realize that Serena has removed herself from the group chat.

I'm already at Serena's front door by the time I read Brianna's latest message. Too late to turn back now. Besides, maybe showing up at Serena's house is exactly what she needs.

One thing's for sure, I need answers.

I press the buzzer and wait.

A moment later, a shadow appears behind the frosted glass and Serena opens the door.

Her dark hair is rumpled, and her eyes look red and tired.

"Hey, Jenna," she murmurs.

"Hey." I give her a hug. "I wasn't sure if you'd want to see anyone, but…"

"I saw you from my window," she says in a fragile voice. "I don't mind if it's just you."

"How are you feeling?"

She shrugs. "Like shit."

"What happened at school yesterday? You left early. Imogen was looking for you at lunch."

"Yeah. I ditched after first period. I couldn't stand being around everyone, all those fakes feeling sorry for me, pretending they actually give a shit." She takes a shaky breath. "You wanna come in?"

I follow her inside. "They do care, Serena. Brianna and Imogen are really worried about you. We all are. Maybe you should text them, just to let them know you're okay."

She scoffs as we head upstairs. "Yeah, everyone's *so* worried. So goddamn worried."

I trail silently behind her, my fingers skimming along the staircase banister.

When we reach her room, Serena sinks onto the bed and pulls a cushion to her chest. "I'm mad at everyone, Jenna. I hate feeling this way, but I'm just so mad. I'm even mad at him."

I close the door and perch on the edge of her bed. "Who? Max?"

"Yeah."

"Well, you're grieving." I gaze around at the balled-up tissues on the nightstand and floor. "I'm sure feeling angry is part of that. It's a healing process."

She grimaces. "I keep replaying conversations we had, things he did..."

"Like what?"

"The bad stuff, y'know? The bad stuff that we never resolved. I can't fix it now. *He* can't fix it now."

I hold her gaze. "What bad stuff?"

She sucks in her top lip. "Max cheated."

The comment makes me freeze.

Oh my god. My heart starts beating a little faster. Serena knows about Max and Colleen. This means that either Imogen has told her since yesterday, or...

"Yep," she says, sizing up my expression. "He cheated on me. And I didn't tell anyone because I was too embarrassed." She rubs roughly at her eyes. "Like it was my fault or something."

I gather my spiraling thoughts. "I'm sorry," I murmur.

A bitter laugh escapes her lips. "I thought, if this gets out, if people find out, then they'll think it's me. They'll think that I'm not good enough for him. That I'm too boring to be with a Rook."

"That's not true. No one would have thought that."

"But they would have. All those vultures at school. You know what they say about people, how they talk. I'd have been the joke of Preston."

"You could have told me."

She shakes her head. "I couldn't tell anyone, Jenna. It was easier that way. It was easier to pretend it wasn't real. I didn't want to believe that Max could do that to me. But he did."

I stare down at the carpet for a second. "How did you find out?"

"Colleen told me." A tear spills from her eye and rolls onto her cheek. "I'm sorry, Jenna. I know she's dead and I'm supposed to be all nice about her and everything, but I hated that bitch."

A tsunami of thoughts begin to sweep through my mind. Colleen told Serena? So, Serena knew, this whole time? Colleen *did* manage to get to her, after all.

She knew.

My heart is hammering in my chest.

"Serena." I stumble over my words. "Colleen... Colleen told you on the night she died..."

Her brow creases. "What? No. It was way before then, back in summer."

I press my hand to my brow. "Hold up. I'm confused. Colleen told you about her fling with Max in the summer? I thought it only just happened?"

"What? What do you mean, Colleen's fling with Max?" Her lips part, and with a slow thud in my chest I realize that we're on two totally different pages.

She didn't know.

At least, not about them.

I scramble to find the words to backtrack, but it's too late. It's already out there.

"Max and *Colleen*?" Her voice goes up an octave. "*What*? When?"

"I don't know." I wince. "Right before Colleen was murdered, I think."

Serena chokes out a sob, and I pull her into a hug.

"I'm so sorry. I thought you knew. You just said Colleen told you about—"

"No!" More tears spill from her eyes, and she sucks in a fractured breath. "No, I didn't know. Last summer, Colleen told me that she'd caught Max cheating on me, but she was a total bitch and refused to tell me who it was with!"

Serena's fight with Max before summer break, I suddenly remember. I can picture it like it was yesterday. Serena screaming at Max in the parking lot, Max apologizing all doe-eyed and innocent-looking. I remember it all so clearly. Max had cheated on Serena then, too?

Serena starts breathing fast. Her words are coming out too quickly. "I bet it was her, though. Colleen. I bet it was her, all along. It did cross my mind, you know? At first, I thought maybe it was Hollie—"

"Wait. You thought Hollie hooked up with Max last summer? Our Hollie?"

"Yeah. For a hot minute I did, anyway. Just because of the way Colleen was talking, saying that it was someone we knew and she didn't want to betray their confidence. And Hollie and Colleen were always whispering about guys. That's why I stopped hanging out with you and Hol, just in case it was her."

"Serena," I breathe, "Hollie would never have done that to you."

"Yeah, well, that's exactly what I thought about Max. He swore he'd never do it to me again. After last summer, after I found out. And with freaking Colleen, of all people. Trash."

"You think it was Colleen both times?"

"I'll bet," Serena rasps through gritted teeth. "I *knew* Colleen was into him. She was always so needy, creeping around him, showing up at the cabin like anyone actually wanted her there. I've always hated her, and now I know that I was right to."

"Serena, I'm so sorry…"

"I hate him." She chokes out the words between sobs. "I hate him for doing this to me. *Again.*"

I hand her a tissue from the box on the nightstand.

I think I just made things a whole lot worse.

★ ★ ★

"Oh my god," Hollie says. "She is losing it. She's totally losing it."

I peer over the top of my sunglasses from the safety of the quad. "We shouldn't be watching this. We should give them some privacy."

"Um, privacy? Jenna, they're in the middle of the parking lot. Everyone can see this."

Dozens of Preston-plaid girls have already flocked to watch the spectacle of Serena yelling at her Rook boyfriend and him looking remorseful as he tries to grasp for her hand.

"Still." I gnaw on my lower lip. "I don't think we should be out here watching this, Hol. It's making me uncomfortable."

"I really don't think Serena cares who's watching at this point."

Through the crowds of onlookers huddled together on the quad, I spot Colleen, Brianna, and Imogen making their way toward us.

Colleen is smirking. "Enjoying the matinee, ladies? Your girl Serena is batshit!"

"Seriously," Imogen says, shaking her head. "Do you guys have any idea what this is about?"

"Nope. None." I'm still watching the fight out of the corner of my eye. We all are. It's a total train wreck. Every now and then, Serena's voice goes up an octave, and Max tosses out another weak apology.

"I think it's just some drama over Max talking to other girls," Brianna says. "Typical Serena, overreacting."

Colleen's gaze wanders away from us. "Yeah. Drama."

"We shouldn't be talking like this," I mutter. "We shouldn't be watching."

Brianna taps her finger on her lips. "I think it's okay," she says. "It's in the parking lot. Ergo, it's public domain."

Colleen laughs.

Through the crowd, I see Serena stalk away from Max, leaving him alone in the parking lot. Her long black hair is swishing behind her as she heads for the school building.

"I'm going to go talk to Max," Colleen says, and she heads toward the lot.

Imogen hurries off after Serena, and Brianna hovers between following Imogen or Colleen, before deciding to chase after Max as he heads for the Dodge he drove here in.

"We should go find Serena," I say to Hollie.

She shakes her head. "No. Let Imogen go. We'll just crowd her. She won't want to talk to us right now."

I frown. "Hollie, we're her best friends. Whatever's gone on, she'll need support."

"Not from us. Come on, let's just go to the cafeteria. We'll see Serena later, after everything's died down." Her gaze travels back to the parking lot as the Dodge tears out onto the road.

ADAM

My dad calls in the afternoon. I'd been expecting it. Since I'm involved in a murder investigation, he doesn't have much choice.

It'd look bad if he didn't.

I almost send the call to voice mail, but I lose my nerve.

With my phone pressed to my ear, I stand on a flat rock on Rookwood Beach and stare out to the horizon. My eyes stay trained on the ocean as he speaks.

"Adam." The familiarity of Dad's voice hits me somewhere in my rib cage. I can practically smell the cut grass and barley and hear the sound of his work boots crunching over gravel. "The school called me."

"Yeah. I figured they would."

"What happened, son?"

Son. There's that damn word again. It has no place in my vocabulary. I'm no one's son. Not anymore.

"A kid died. Someone drove my car into the harbor."

"Who drove your car, Adam?" He's getting frustrated. I

can hear it in his clipped words and sharp breaths. He gets like this whenever I don't have the answers for him, or when he can't figure out how to patch over my issues. I want to hang up. I want to tell him that he gave up his right to get angry the day he walked out on my mom and me. Or the day he signed the papers to send me here.

The day he gave up on me, right after we buried my mother.

But I don't. I just answer his question. "I don't know. Someone took my keys. The cops are looking into it."

Another terse breath down the line. "You weren't driving that car?"

"Nope."

"The police believe that?"

"Nope."

"Adam, if you and your friends are caught up in something…" He trails off.

I don't see much point in responding.

"You're going to need a lawyer," he mutters.

"Yeah. I know."

He exhales heavily. I'm struggling to remember the last time I spoke to him. He called around Christmastime when I didn't come home. We spoke. The usual formalities, *How are you? Fine. How are you?* All that bullshit. He called again on my birthday; the conversation went the same way. Today is different, though. Today is the first time we've spoken like *this*—heated, tense, raw.

I can't do it. If I let myself go there, if I let myself *feel* anything, I won't be able to come back from it.

I'm not strong enough.

So I tell him I've got it covered, and then I end the call. Staring out at the gray horizon, I clench my teeth so hard that I swear I taste blood.

JENNA

Kate steps into my bedroom and perches on the edge of my bed. "Okay, spill."

I drop my phone into my lap and force a smile. "What do you mean?"

"You've been moping around the house all evening. All week, actually. What's up with you?"

I draw in a breath. "Nothing. I'm fine."

"Is this about the fight we had? About you spending time at Rookwood?"

I swallow hard.

There's a hint of a smile on her lips. "Hold up. Is this the teenage rebellious phase I've been hearing so much about? Are you planning on slamming doors and yelling about how I'm not your mom? And there was me thinking I'd dodged all that fun."

"Sorry to disappoint you, but I don't think I'll be slamming any doors today. You're right about Rookwood. I should never have gone."

"But you did." She's picking me apart with her gaze.

"Yeah."

"Want to elaborate? I get the feeling there's more to this story than what you're telling me."

I press my hands together.

"Jenna," she says, "I know I'm not your mom, but you can talk to me. I mean, damn, if you can't talk to me after three years then I've really screwed up this whole parenting thing, haven't I?" She musters a laugh, but there's real tension in her expression.

"Kate, don't say that. You've been the best aunt-slash-mom-type-person I could ever ask for."

"Well, now I know you're lying," she says. I frown at her, and she adds, "I haven't been around much. I realize that. I have no idea what's been going on with you. I figure that's a pretty big sign that I've let you down."

"You haven't let me down. Not at all. You've had to work. I understand."

She reaches across the bed and pats my leg. "But that all needs to change. It's going to change. Consider this your official grilling from your aunt-slash-mom-type-person. Talk to me. What's going on?"

Good question. I wish I knew.

"Go on," Kate says. "You have my complete, undivided attention."

I rub my brow. Honestly, I don't know where to begin. Or if I should be telling her anything at all. She'll flip if she finds out how much information I've been keeping from her.

But I need to talk to someone I can trust. Someone who isn't involved with Max or Colleen or Rookwood. I feel like

I'm drifting, and I need an anchor. Kate feels like my only lifeline right now.

"Adam." I say his name and instantly feel like I'm betraying him.

Kate's brow creases. "Adam Cole? What about him?"

"Is he a suspect?"

Concern lines her face. "Why do you ask?" She's searching my eyes. "I mean, I know that you know him. But how *well* do you know him?"

My voice goes quiet. "Reasonably well."

Kate blinks at me a couple of times, like she's struggling to process this bombshell. Her non-door-slamming, drama-free niece and a potential suspect in a double homicide. Awesome.

The question slips from my mouth. "Do you think he killed Max?"

"I can't answer that."

"Colleen?" I press.

She gives way to a long sigh. "Jenna, you know I can't answer these questions."

"But what do you think? Kate, this is important. I have to know. Am I reading him all wrong? I saw how Serena was with Max, totally blinded by him. Is that me?"

"You're not Serena."

"Aren't I?"

Kate gazes down at her hands. She laces her fingers together. "You want to know what I think?" she says at last.

"Yes. Please."

"I think you're a smart girl," she says. "And I think you already know the answer."

ADAM

I sit on the rocks in the darkness, just listening to the tide. It murmurs to me.

There's a crunch of sand and click of pebbles as she approaches. I don't know why she's here. I didn't call her. I haven't in days.

But I know it's her before she even comes close.

Her silhouette moves through the moonlight. Arms wrapped around herself, shielding her from the night wind. Or from me.

"Hi," I say as she sits beside me on the sand.

"Hi."

There's a pause between us, and the tide murmurs again.

"I'm sorry." Her words merge with the sounds of the ocean.

"Don't be."

"It's been a couple of days," she says, softly. "I should have called or texted. Something."

"I've missed you." That's probably the most honest thing I've ever said to her. To anyone.

"I've missed you, too."

I don't know if anyone has ever missed me before.

She catches my gaze. "How have you been?"

My shoulders tighten. I think of my dad. Our phone conversation. Blood rushes to my head, and I exhale to make it go away.

"Alright," I tell her. "The cops are coming back to talk to me first thing in the morning. I figured I'd spend tonight out here. Just in case they bring me in tomorrow."

She turns away. She won't meet my eyes.

"How have you been?" I return the question.

"Confused, mostly."

"Yeah. I didn't expect you to come back. I thought you'd be done with me by now, after everything that's happened." I dig my sneaker into the hard sand. "I know it doesn't look good."

"I'm glad you were here." She pauses and shivers, then rubs her hands up and down her arms for warmth. It's getting colder now. The change has been brewing for a while. "I made a dumb mistake, Adam. I should have trusted my instincts. I should have trusted you."

"Yeah?"

Her hand folds around mine. "I *do* trust you."

A strange laugh escapes my lips. "Thanks."

Her eyes are back on me now, and I feel my walls crumbling. It's my turn to look away from her. I turn my attention to the dark water as it rushes against the shore. Moonlight dances on the surface. The moon is waning now. I can't see the faint outline of the crescent that isn't there, but it's still whole, somewhere. "I know what people say about me."

She threads her fingers through mine and stays silent.

"They don't know me, though."

"I know you."

"I hope you do. I want you to."

She smiles gently in the darkness.

"It wasn't my fault," I mutter. "I didn't know how to help her."

There's a pause between us while she untangles my words. "You mean, your mom?" she asks.

My mind's back there now. It's as though the bolted doors are creaking open and I'm falling right back into the abyss. I'm back in that barley field, on the porch. She's on the ground, choking, convulsing. I'm twelve years old again, and all I can do is stare. I can't move. I can't think. I don't know what to do. I don't know how to save her.

I'm not even sure that I want to.

I blink, and just like that I'm back on Rookwood Beach with Jenna. Only now, I have that thought, that memory. I can taste it. I lived it all over again. Bile rises in my throat.

"She was an addict." My voice is weak, scratchy, betraying the secrets of where I've just been. "She OD'd. I found her, but I didn't know what to do. So I did nothing. I just stood there. It must have been about ten minutes before I even managed to call 911." Pain floods through me, everywhere. My eyes. My chest. My heart. Just saying those words aloud makes everything hurt.

Jenna rests her head on my shoulder. "I'm so sorry," she whispers.

"My dad came back on the scene after that. He had to, I was just a kid. But I lost it. I kind of spiraled for a little while. I started acting out, self-destructing, and my dad couldn't deal with me anymore. The cops stepped in. They called social services, and the next thing I knew, I was here." My eyes travel over the rocky shore. "The other guys here don't know about what happened. Only Tommy and Max."

She's looking at me, waiting for more. The mention of Max has made her fingers tighten around mine.

"Max understood," I say. "There were people in his family who were addicts. He got it. Anyway, he told one of the Preston girls about my mom one night. I guess it was Colleen. He came clean to me, though, said he'd had too much to drink and it just came out. We were cool after. But it didn't matter, it was too late."

"But you didn't kill your mom." Her voice is soft. "You must have told Max that."

"Yeah. Maybe he got the story wrong. Or maybe those girls who found out figured I must have killed her for the cops to intervene. Things must have gotten seriously messed up for me to have been sent here. Anyway, looks like the rumor is out now." I turn to Jenna, and she's with me, completely. "They didn't see the years I spent watching her fade away after my dad left. They don't know the guilt that eats away at me. They just see the guy who watched her die."

"That's not who you are."

"No. But it's a part of my story. It made me who I am."

She sighs. "Who you are is a caring and loyal guy. Your mom would have been proud of you. Your dad should be, too."

A hollow sound escapes my throat.

Her hand moves along my arm, and then her lips find mine in the darkness.

I pull her closer to me. "Thank you for coming back."

"Thank you for being here when I did."

IMOGEN: Hey, girls. Has anyone heard from Serena? I'm pretty sure she blocked me. I really don't know what I've done wrong.

BRIANNA: Drop it already, Ims! If Serena doesn't want to talk to you, that's her problem. Wanna go out tonight?

IMOGEN: Jenna? What do you think about the Serena situation? Update me.

JENNA: She's just in a really tough place right now. Don't take it personally.

IMOGEN: Has she talked to you, though?

BRIANNA: Imogen! Seriously! We don't even like Serena!

JENNA

I open Colleen's Instagram page. The comments on her posts have stopped now. It's like she's slipping into a hazy memory. There are fewer *miss you!* comments. Fewer *so sad!* comments. Now, there are just frozen pictures and distant dates.

But I'm not here to read the comments. I need to go further back. Back to the pictures taken before Colleen was murdered.

As my eyes wander over the photos, I start to notice details. Details that I didn't pay attention to before. Like Max, for example. There's only one shot of Colleen with Max. Her arm is draped around his neck, and she's gazing blearily at him. But he's looking away from her.

He's looking at someone else.

I move on to Max's profile next. It's mostly shots of him. Some alone, some with Serena, some with Adam or the other Rooks. Everything's kind of generic. Just a normal guy, doing normal things.

But there's one common thread in dozens of the pictures: there's someone in the background. She's hovering just within the boundaries of the frame. Blond hair caught in the camera's flash. Eyes lingering on him.

She's watching him. And a lot of the time, he's watching her too.

It hits me all of a sudden. I've been wrong.

All this time, I've been wrong about everything.

Finger marks, that's what the police had found as possible evidence. They were looking at the finger marks of a *female*. I'm sure of it.

I listen for movement in the house. Kate is asleep, her bedroom across the hall is silent.

I scroll through my Contacts list and press Call.

ADAM

My phone lights up the darkness of the dorm room. Jenna's name is on the screen.

I glance at Tommy. He's breathing steadily under the covers. He's been asleep for a while.

Grabbing my phone, I stand and step into the corridor. I close the door quietly behind me and hit answer.

"Hey."

"Hey," her voice comes back to me. "Did I wake you?"

"No." I scrub my hand through my hair. "I was already awake."

She hesitates.

"Is everything okay?"

She takes a quick breath. "You said Max was seeing Colleen behind Serena's back."

"Yeah."

"Are you sure? Are you sure it was Colleen?"

My brow furrows as I stare along the dimly lit corridor. "Yeah. Of course."

"How do you know for sure?"

"She said it." I lower my voice. "Colleen threatened him that night. I told you that already."

"Yes, but what did Colleen say, exactly?"

I drag my mind back to that Friday night in the cabin, the last time any of us saw Colleen alive. "I'm going to tell Serena exactly what you've been doing behind her back." I echo her words. They're burned into my memory now. Just like she is.

"Did Max ever directly tell you that he was cheating on Serena with Colleen?"

"We knew he was. He was acting shady. He used to talk about a girl. A girl who wasn't Serena."

"He used to talk about Colleen? He actually said her name?"

I have to think back. Ever since the night Colleen disappeared, everything has blurred and skewed. "No," I say to Jenna. "No. He never mentioned her name."

"So," she says, letting out a tense breath, "what if it wasn't Colleen?"

It takes me a moment to catch up with her train of thought. "You mean, what if Colleen found out he was cheating on Serena with someone *else* and threatened him?"

I'm going to tell Serena exactly what you've been doing behind her back.

"Could be, right?"

"Colleen was mad that night." I piece together my scattered memories. "She was really mad."

"So, maybe she knew about Max cheating with someone, and she was threatening to tell Serena. That would explain why things got so heated. In their own strange way, Colleen and Serena were actually friends. I don't know, maybe Colleen felt a moral duty to tell Serena."

I have to catch myself. It's not only Colleen who isn't around to ask anymore. Max isn't around, either. Sometimes, I have to remind myself of that. "I don't think Max would have told me the truth about this anyway," I say aloud, and the realization stings a bit. "He was covering something up. I know he was."

Max was covering his secret.

Just like Tommy covered his.

And I tried to cover mine.

"You still don't think Max killed Colleen?" Jenna's voice jolts me back.

"No. But he knew who did."

When she doesn't respond, my grip tightens around my phone. "Jenna?"

"Yes," she murmurs. "I'm still here."

"Where's your head at?"

"Max cheated on Serena last summer as well. Do you know who it was with?"

My eyes wander over the empty corridor. Everything's quiet. Everything's dark. "No. I didn't know about that."

"Serena said it was with a friend. Could it be the same girl this time around?"

"What, and Max has been seeing her since the summer? And Colleen found out?"

She's breathing fast. "It's a possibility, right?"

"Yeah." I remember the faraway look in Max's eyes when he spoke about the girl he'd fallen for. The girl who wasn't Serena.

"If Colleen threatened to expose them, and then Max was going to come clean to Serena last week…"

"That's twice she could have been caught out."

"Maybe the same girl is behind both murders."

I rub the nape of my neck. "You think someone would care that much about screwing Serena over? Kill two people rather than get called out as a home wrecker?"

"No. I think there's a lot more to it than that."

I gaze up at the shadows on the ceiling. "Right. You said this girl from the summer was a friend of Serena's?"

"Yes."

"But you don't know who?"

"I have a pretty good idea."

"The girl who everyone blamed?" Jenna falters when I say the name out loud. "Hollie."

JENNA

I hear the commotion before I even step into the cafeteria.

Girls have already flocked around the lunch tables, trying to get the best view of the catfight taking place at our table.

I push my way through the crowd.

Hollie is at the center of it.

"Whoa! What's going on?"

Hollie points a trembling finger at Colleen. "Ask her!"

Colleen smirks. "I don't know what this bitch is talking about."
Compared to Hollie, Colleen doesn't even look fazed. She's leaning back in her seat, sipping soda through a straw.

"Liar!" Hollie screams. "You knew how much I liked him, and you still went after him."

Colleen blinks back at her, all doe-eyed and guiltless. "Who?"

"You know who!"

I place my hand on Hollie's arm. "Come on, Hol. Calm down."
I glance around at the circus of hungry onlookers. This is not a fight that needs to happen in the Preston cafeteria. The social leeches will be all over this.

Hollie's jaw clenches. "You're a snake, Colleen. You really are."

Her hands flutter to her chest. "Who, me?"

I hold Hollie's arm a little tighter.

"Listen, Hol," Colleen says, "whatever you think I did, you're wrong. I don't do sloppy seconds. You got that?"

"Then why is there a picture of you draped all over him?"

"Excuse you, stalker. I'm not a skank. I didn't kiss your boy. Or your wannabe boy, whatever."

Hollie glares at her. "If I find out you have, I swear..."

Colleen stands up at the challenge. "Yeah? You'll what?"

"I'll kill you!"

"Yeah. Whatever, bitch." Colleen flips her hair and turns away.

Interview with Hollie Braithwaite,
conducted by Detective Kate Dallas at 9:05 a.m.
on Monday, October 1st.

K.D.: Let's get straight to the point, Hollie. How did you know Colleen O'Dell?

H.B.: She was my friend. I've known her since middle school.

K.D.: You girls were close?

H.B.: We were friends.

K.D.: I heard that you and Colleen had quite some argument the day before she was found. You want to tell me about that?

H.B.: What? What do you mean?

K.D.: I think you know what I mean, Hollie.

H.B.: Oh. Yes. I think so. But it wasn't even really an argument. Not really.

K.D.: That's not what your classmates are saying.

K.D.: Hollie? Want to try this again? Tell me about the fight you had with Colleen O'Dell on Friday, September twenty-eighth.

H.B.: It was nothing. Colleen and I both liked the same guy. But it was nothing serious. It was nothing. Honestly. We were fine. We were all good again, like, five minutes later. I swear.

K.D.: Who was this boy you were fighting over?

H.B.: Just a boy we hang out with sometimes. He's a student at Rookwood.

K.D.: I'm going to need a name.

H.B.: His name's Scotch. I mean, Tyler Scotch.

ADAM

"Dad. What are you doing here?"

"Adam. I've been trying to call you." He paces toward me from across the courtyard. The sun is rising over the treetops, throwing strips of light across the ground.

I pat my pockets. "I must have left my cell in the dorm."

I'm trying to remember the last time I saw him. A year ago, maybe? I don't see him at behavior management meetings. I know he comes, but I don't see him.

He looks the same, but older, grayer. There are more lines around his eyes.

We face each other in the courtyard as the morning breeze drags through the trees.

"How are you?" he asks.

I shake my head.

"How can I help?" he presses. "What do you need?"

"A miracle would be nice."

"I found a lawyer." He takes a crumpled flyer from his shirt pocket and shows it to me. A middle-aged woman dressed in a power suit glowers at me from the glossy paper. Her inked face is faded in parts from where the flyer has been folded. "She's good. She has a great track record for cases like this. We can fix this."

"This isn't your problem, Dad. I do alright on my own. I always have."

He grimaces. "This is serious, Adam. Why didn't you tell me the police are coming here to question you today? I had to hear it from your principal."

"It's not a big deal." I take the flyer and inspect it a little closer. There's a whole load of small print at the bottom. Dial-a-Lawyer kind of shit.

"It is a big deal. They might arrest you, Adam. Do you understand that?"

"Yeah. I've done this before. Remember?"

His eyes move away from mine. And we're right back to where we were a year ago. Distant. Guarded.

I grit my teeth. "Why are you here, Dad?"

"To help you. You need my help."

I laugh under my breath.

"Adam," he says. "I'm trying. Give me something. Talk to me."

"You want me to talk?"

"Please."

"Alright." I take a ragged breath. "Do you think I did it?" The words come out fast.

"Of course not. That's why I'm here, to help straighten this damn mess out."

"No. I didn't mean that." I hesitate for a beat. "Do you think I killed Mom?" The sound of the words unleashed into the empty courtyard make my stomach turn.

"No," he murmurs. "No, you didn't kill your mother."

I'm silent, just still, listening to the whispers of the ghosts that haunt us.

"She was an addict," he says. "She had a sickness, and she couldn't get a handle on it. None of that was your fault."

"You sent me here. Right after Mom died, you showed up out of nowhere, and you sent me here. Do you know how much that screwed me up?"

He runs a calloused hand over his face. "I was in over my head," he mutters. "I didn't know how to be a dad. I still don't."

"I was just a kid."

"I know. You think I don't regret what happened back then?"

"Honestly?" I hold his stare. "No. No, I don't think you regret it at all."

"I thought you'd have a better chance here, at this school." He gestures to the looming gothic building behind us. "There are opportunities for you. I thought you'd be better off here than wasting away on the goddamn farm with me and the memories of your mom."

I think of the scholarship, the chance I could have if I work hard enough to make it a reality. But that was before I became a suspect in a double homicide.

"I'm sorry." His voice is hoarse.

"Yeah." I stuff my hands into my pockets. "Me, too."

"You're my son. I know I screwed up. But you're my son."

I nod. My eyes stray from him and linger on the slowly swaying trees. Truth is, I think I've forgotten how to be a son. But we can start again. Maybe.

He offers his hand, and I shake it. Maybe that's all I need. Maybe that's all I ever needed.

JENNA

I need to talk to you, **I write to Serena.**

My hands are shaking.

There's a monster out there, and I think I know who she is.

The problem is there's only one person who can help me figure out who Max was cheating with last summer. And that's Serena. But she won't take my calls.

I didn't sleep. I spent all night waiting for dawn. Waiting for Serena to wake up and check her messages.

Finally, after a dozen unread texts, a little tick appears alongside the last message I sent to her. She's read it.

The minutes pass by slowly. I keep checking my cell. But there's nothing new from Serena.

I stare at my phone.

Come on, Serena.

I try messaging her again. I really need to talk to you. I know this is hard for you, but I think I know who Max was cheating on you with, and it wasn't Colleen. Please call me.

It takes a few minutes, but finally, Serena's response flashes across my phone's screen.

Can you meet?

Yes, I write back, quickly. Your house?

I'm not there. Meet at the cabin.

I frown at the text message. The Rookwood cabin was locked up by the groundskeeper after what happened to Max. As far as I was aware, it had been boarded shut to stop any more prohibited parties from taking place on the school grounds.

I try calling Serena again, but she doesn't pick up.

Why are you at Rookwood? I type. Can I meet you back at your house? Or at Chai?

She responds. I'm already at the cabin. Meet here. There's no one else around.

That doesn't exactly fill me with optimism. Why are you there?

She doesn't reply. But I guess it makes sense that Serena would want to return to the place where she'd shared most of her memories with Max. Maybe this makes her feel closer to him somehow.

I shrug into my coat and start walking toward Rookwood. I take a shortcut through the forest, fighting through the overgrown branches until I reach the hidden spot where the cabin is concealed.

The entire area has been cordoned off with yellow police

tape that's fluttering in the shallow breeze. The cabin's windows have all been boarded up, and there's more tape crisscrossing the door. Something about this place gives me chills. It seems eerie in the shadows of the bowed trees. Even the air hangs heavily around it, full of ghosts.

"Serena?" I call.

The wind howls back at me, and I shiver. This doesn't feel right. Serious red flags.

I take out my phone and call Kate. It goes straight to voice mail.

"Hey, Kate," I say after the beep. "It's me. Just letting you know that I'm meeting Serena at the Rookwood cabin. Sorry. Don't hate me. I'll explain later."

With a deep breath, I sidestep the overgrown ivy and try the handle on the door. It eases open. I duck beneath the tape and step inside.

The cabin is cold, still scattered with empty bottles and crumpled plastic cups from its last party. I press my coat sleeve to my nose to block the smell of stale cigarette smoke and beer.

There's a muffled cry from across the room.

I spin on my heel.

Serena. Her eyes are wide and wild.

My breath catches in my throat.

She's tied to a chair, and a strip of duct tape is covering her mouth.

ADAM

The cops will be here by now, probably waiting for me in Principal Lomax's office.

I rummage around my side of the dorm room, searching for my cell. Tommy's still in bed. He looks half-asleep, heavy-eyed and yawning, but he's sitting upright.

"Hey." His voice is groggy. "Why are you up so early? Class doesn't start for half an hour."

I shake my bedcover, and my phone thumps to the floor. "I've got a date with the cops," I tell Tommy. "And my dad, apparently."

"What? Why are you meeting the cops?"

"Because they want to bust me for Max."

He sits up straighter. "What? But you gave me as your alibi, right?"

"Nope."

"Why not?"

"Because it's a lie. You're not my alibi."

"So? I'll tell them. I'm coming with you." He moves to stand up, but I stop him.

"Don't get involved, Tommy. I'm not going to drag you into this."

"Adam, come on." He slaps his hand to his brow. "We're in this together. Just like we have been from the start."

I can't bring myself to look at him. "This isn't your problem. If we get caught lying, we'll both be screwed. You know that."

"I'm not going to bail on you."

I glance at him. "She has a theory, you know."

He blinks back at me. "Who?"

"Jenna."

Tommy shakes his head, confused. "A theory about what?"

"About Max, Colleen, everything."

There's silence while he waits for me to elaborate.

"Max cheated on Serena last summer. Did you know about that?"

He runs a hand over his brow. "No, but I'm not exactly surprised."

"Yeah. Well, it's looking like he cheated with one of Serena's friends. One of the Preston girls."

He nods slowly.

I pause, thinking about Max and the last time I saw him alive. I swallow against a burning sensation in my throat when I remember our last conversation, only a couple of hours before his body was pulled from the water. He was drunk that night, yeah, but he was in control. He wasn't high. He never was. And damn sure he wasn't so wasted that he couldn't get out of a sinking car.

"Did you sell anything to Max on Friday night?" I ask Tommy.

"Nothing. You know Max wouldn't touch the stuff anyway."

"What about the girls? Did you sell anything to any of the girls who were here that night?"

He stares back at me. His jaw tenses. "You think someone drugged Max?"

"They must have, right? Why wouldn't he get out of a sinking car, Tommy? He must have been on something. Something strong enough to knock him out cold."

Tommy rubs his brow. He mutters something under his breath.

My pulse quickens. "What?"

"One of the girls bought something off me. But I swear it was the last of my stash. I was just trying to get rid of it all. I was going to stop selling—"

"What did she buy?"

His eyes squeeze shut for a second. "Rohypnol."

I feel like my heart just dropped through the floorboards. "Tommy..."

"I know," he mutters. "I'm sorry. I know."

My voice comes out in a rasp. "You were selling a date-rape drug to people?"

"My dad..." He's stuttering now, fumbling. "My dad needed me to sell it. But I was only giving it to some of the guys with insomnia, just to help them sleep, I swear, not to..."

My skin crawls at the thought.

"It was the last of it," he says. "I was going to stop. You've got to believe me, Adam. I never meant for Max... I never thought that anyone would give it to Max. *Shit.*"

"Who did you sell it to?"

"There was a girl. I sold it to a girl."

"What was her name?" My mind jumps back to Friday night, before my fight with Max. I remember seeing a girl at the cabin, after Serena had gone home. I remember seeing her before, too, talking to Tommy in the shadows of the room. It was the same girl I once saw Max share a cigarette with while Serena looked on. The same girl that Max couldn't take his eyes off when she walked past us at Colleen's vigil.

"She's a friend of Serena's." Tommy's voice is shaking. "I've seen them together."

"What's her name?"

For Jenna's sake, I pray he doesn't say Hollie.

And he doesn't.

I try calling Jenna. But she doesn't pick up.

JENNA

Someone grabs my hair from behind. My phone hits the floor and skids across the planks. Out the corner of my eye, I see Adam's name flash across the screen as it rings.

But I'm gripped by a searing pain as the person behind me pulls me to the ground. My palms hit the floorboards with a smack.

Across the room, Serena is hysterical. Tears are spilling down her cheeks, but her sobs are muffled behind the tape covering her mouth.

I know whose hands are pressing down on me, restraining me. I know because I saw her. It wasn't Colleen gazing adoringly at Max in the photos. Or Hollie fixating on the mystery Rook guy she'd met at a party.

In every photo, this girl's eyes were trained on him. I saw it, her unwavering purpose captured in the still frame.

"Imogen," I say. "Let us go."

She flinches at my voice and loosens her grip for a second. It's long enough for me to struggle free of her and grab my phone. But it's only a moment before I feel a smack to my skull. A dull ache spreads across the back of my head. My cell slips from my hand and hits the floor again. The screen blurs as my eyes lose focus.

I'm pushed back down to the floor. In my foggy vision, the pool table spins, Serena turns fuzzy, and all I see clearly is Imogen standing over me. I blink fast, trying to focus on only her, trying to drown out Serena's stifled cries.

"Imogen," I manage again. "You can't do this. You have to let us out of here."

"No." Her voice is trembling. "No, Jenna. I can't."

The color has drained from her face, and she's shaking. I've never seen her look so out of control—perfect, pretty Imogen is gone. She's holding a glass vase, and she lifts it a little higher.

I shrink back. One more hit with that and it's over for me.

"Imogen, please…"

"I had to get you both here." She starts rambling, muttering almost to herself. "It's the only way I can make this work."

I draw in a rough breath. "Make what work?"

"Does anyone else know?" She's panting, blond hair flying across her face, disturbed by the rasps of her breath. "You have to tell me. I need to know the names of anyone else who knows."

I stare back at her, trying to find my voice through my fear.

"You knew…" She aims her index finger at me. "And now *she* knows." Imogen gestures to Serena. "Who else knows about Max and me?"

I shake my head. "No one."

"Did you tell your aunt? Adam?"

"No. I don't know anything, Imogen. Whatever you think—"

"You don't understand. Colleen was going to tell Serena."

Her voice warbles with the words. "Colleen found out about us, and she was going to tell Serena."

I take a quick breath. "She caught you last summer, didn't she? Colleen caught you and Max together?"

Her fingers clench on the vase.

I forge on. "But your relationship with Max didn't end then?" I already know the answer.

"You don't understand," she whispers.

I say quickly, "Talk to me, Imogen. I get it. I can only imagine how hard it must have been for you, having to watch Serena and Max together. Your fling with Max didn't end last summer, did it?"

Her eyes snap to me. "It wasn't a fling, Jenna."

"Then what was it? A few hookups? A secret relationship?"

Her jaw tightens. "He was mine," she murmurs. "He was always supposed to be mine."

Serena lets out a stifled scream.

Imogen's words hang in the air, and goose bumps spread along my arms.

"You knew him," I murmur. Suddenly the missing pieces start to fit. "You told me that. You told me you knew Max from your neighborhood. You two went to school together, before Preston and Rookwood."

Her lips part, and her eyes glaze over as though she's suddenly lost in the past. "Even after Max was sent to Rookwood, I still thought about him sometimes. I just didn't realize how I felt about him until it was too late."

"Too late?" I ball my hands to stop them from shaking. "You mean, because he was already in love with Serena?"

Her eyebrows pinch together. "He didn't love her," she seethes through her teeth. "I know he didn't. Max and I, we're from the same world. Serena could never compete with that. It was real with us. It was inevitable." She bites her lower lip. "It was intense."

"So how come Max didn't just break up with Serena last summer? Then the two of you wouldn't have had to hide anymore."

Imogen's focus jumps back to me. "It wasn't that simple." She starts pacing in small circles, her footsteps tapping fast on the floorboards. "Serena was his free ride out of this shithole town. He needed her. That bitch Colleen almost ruined everything for him."

I manage another uneven breath. "So that's why you killed Colleen, to keep her quiet?"

"No!" Imogen stops pacing. She's trembling. "No, it wasn't like that. Colleen caught Max and I together in the forest, again. I tried to run, but Max called me and told me that Colleen had seen me and was going to talk this time, so I went after her. I just wanted to reason with her. I'd worked so hard to keep this quiet, for Max's sake. For his future—our future."

Serena chokes out another bitter sound.

"You killed Colleen." My words sound hollow. "You had to stop her before she got to Serena?"

Imogen shakes her head, and her ice-blond hair falls limply over her face. "Colleen was *my* friend, not Serena's. I found her on the cliff path, and I tried talking to her. But she was just being so stubborn. She was going to tell Serena everything. There was nothing I could do to stop her."

My voice sounds hoarse as it leaves my lips. "But there was something you could do. There was something you did."

She shifts the weight of the vase in her hands, and I flinch on reflex. "It was an accident. Colleen and I got into a fight.

She told me I was trash for doing this to Serena, and she pushed me, so I pushed her back. It just...escalated."

I wince, my eyes still locked on the vase. If Imogen was capable of grabbing Colleen by the throat and pushing her from Rookwood cliff, I have no doubt she'd bring that vase down over my head if I dare to make one wrong move. But I can't stop now. I have to keep going. "And Max?" I press on. "What happened to Max, Imogen?"

Her eyes skate over Serena again. "I never meant to hurt him," she whispers. "We were soul mates."

With that, Serena starts thrashing her body, kicking her legs and throwing her shoulders in an attempt to break free from the cable ties binding her wrists. The chair rocks with her.

"Imogen." I draw her eyes back to me. "What happened to Max?"

"He was going to end it." All of a sudden, her wild blue eyes glisten, and her voice fractures with emotion. "Last weekend. He told me that one of Serena's friends had found out about us and he was going to be honest with Serena. He felt guilty about everything, and he was going to choose her." A single tear rolls down her cheek. "It was *your* fault," she spits at me. "You were the one who found out. If it wasn't for you, Max would still be here."

Of course she'd known that it was me. That's why I'd had a text from Imogen in the early hours of the morning, asking where I was. Max had told her. Was he already dead by then? Was her plan to move on to me next?

I shuffle backward until my spine is pressed up against the sofa. "I only knew that Max had cheated," I fumble. "I never had your name."

"Serena was on to me. I know she was," Imogen says, blink-

308 · GABRIELLA LEPORE

ing fast. "She was freezing me out. That's why I asked her to meet me here last night. I wouldn't have gotten you involved, Jenna. But then I read that text message you sent to Serena this morning." She dips her gaze, and her long eyelashes sweep downward. "This has to end here, with the two of you."

The back of my head is throbbing, and I can feel something trickling down the nape of my neck—blood. Everything is starting to feel foggy. I clench my teeth, fighting to stay conscious.

She sucks in her cheeks. "What happened to Max wasn't my fault."

"I know," I manage. "I believe you, Imogen."

"Max wanted to talk." Her words start coming out faster, her eyes darting from left to right as she relived the memory in her mind. "Just the two of us. So we went to Adam's car."

My heart feels as though it's about to beat out of my chest. "Were you guys high?"

"I gave Max a little something to relax him, in a drink. He was so stressed out, and I had to buy some time. I knew he was pulling away from me. Ever since Colleen…"

"Did he know what you did?" My hands press down on the floorboards as I struggle to keep myself upright. "Did Max know what happened with Colleen?"

"No. But I think he suspected." She starts gnawing on her lip. "He must have because that's when it all went wrong. He started to pull away from me after that. After Colleen." She rests her brow on the vase and chokes out a sob. "He knew, and it ruined everything."

I swallow hard. "That's why you drugged Max, to stop him from coming clean to Serena?"

"No!" Her face screws up, and she shakes the memory

away. "I didn't mean to give him much. Just enough to calm him down. He was so freaked out about you knowing he'd been cheating. But then he started to get really out of it..."

I cringe at the sound of Serena's cries. "He passed out in Adam's car?"

"It was too much. Way too much." Imogen's hands tighten around the glass vase, her fingers turning white from the force with which she's gripping it. Across the cabin, Serena is suddenly quiet, apart from her quick, shallow breaths. I still can't bring myself to look at her. I can't bring myself to break eye contact with Imogen. I'm afraid that the second I do, that vase will come down onto my skull.

"You drove Adam's car into the harbor," I murmur.

"Max was going to tell Serena about Colleen catching us together. That would have made me a suspect, Jenna. I would have gone down for it. Gotten a life sentence. It was an accident!"

My breath falters. "So you drove the car into the harbor, swam free, and left Max to drown."

She stares back at me, vacant. Her voice becomes hoarse. "It was an accident."

I grope for a response, but nothing comes out.

"Shit," Imogen rasps. "*Shit.* I have to end this." She takes a step closer to me and raises the vase.

"Imogen, no." I shrink back, bracing myself. "You can't kill us. Four victims? You'll get caught."

"I won't. I haven't so far. Everyone will think he did it."

My eyebrows pull together. "Who?"

"Your guy. Adam. The one who killed his mom. Max told me all about it one night when he was drunk. Adam must be a little unhinged, and it was his car. It's obvious that he drove

Max into the harbor. No one will even question it. No one questioned it when I leaked Hollie's text messages, and no one would question Adam driving his *own* car, right?"

"No, Imogen," I whisper. "Please don't do this."

"This is why I had to get you and Serena here together. I'm going to say Adam was hooking up with Serena. And everyone knows he was having a thing with you. I'll say I heard you and Serena talking about a three-way with him, here, last night. His DNA is already everywhere. And, oops, he killed you both." She holds her fingers like a gun.

"Don't do this," I plead.

"Too late. It's already done." She takes a step closer to me and raises the vase. "Sorry, Jenna."

I squeeze my eyes shut.

Suddenly, there are voices outside. Footsteps crunch through the undergrowth.

It feels as though time has slowed down, just for a moment. I watch, frozen, as Imogen drops the vase and it shatters on the floor. I cover my eyes as shards of glass explode around us.

When I lower my hands, Imogen is silent. Her lips are parted. She's breathing quickly as the voices get closer. She turns, and she runs. The door thumps shut behind her.

I slump to the floor.

My eyes are focused now, and this time, when I look at my phone lying just out of arm's reach, the screen isn't blurry. It worked, just like I'd hoped. Adam's name is at the top, my call was answered, and the seconds keep ticking by.

ADAM

I don't know if I believe in luck. For me, most things can boil down to coincidence. But if I ever find myself looking for a definition of *lucky*, I'll think back to the time Tommy and I were right outside Principal Lomax's office, about to be questioned in connection with a double homicide, at the exact moment I needed to play a call on loudspeaker. Luck? Coincidence? Whatever it was, it saved lives.

They caught Imogen a couple of miles from Rookwood. She was found within an hour. I figure that's pretty good police work.

Time has passed since then, just like it always does. But I'm back here again. Back on Rookwood Beach.

Jenna stands beside me, her eyes trained on the crashing waves.

We're right back where we started. Only, we're different now. Stronger.

All of a sudden, she rises to her tiptoes and kisses me.

A smile tugs at my mouth. "What was that for?"

"Just felt like it." She grins. "Also, you looked like you needed it."

"Yeah?" I drape my arm around her shoulders, pulling her closer.

She rests her hand on my heart.

Behind us, pebbles crunch and clink. We both turn to see Tommy and Chris crossing the beach.

Chris. Tommy's boyfriend.

"Hey," I call to them.

They join us at the shoreline. Chris folds his hand around Tommy's, and Tommy glances at me, like he's checking to see if I'm good with this.

I smile back, hoping that's enough for him to know that it's all good. It was always all good.

His shoulders relax.

I breathe a little easier knowing he's happy. Tommy made some dumb mistakes, sure. He never meant to hurt anyone, though. He got off easy with community service, but he still has to live with selling those drugs to Imogen. But Imogen has to live with giving them to Max.

A flock of blackbirds fly over the horizon. Rooks, maybe. They're soaring free, in perfect harmony with each other.

It makes me think of my Rooks, and our brotherhood.

Max is gone. My mom is gone, too.

But I've still got a future ahead of me. And maybe even a scholarship to law school, if I work hard enough. Preferably somewhere with a great photography program nearby.

Me, Jenna, Tommy, Serena, Hollie... We've still got our lives to live, and every chance ahead of us. Because we're the lucky ones.

And from now on, I'm going to make it count.

★ ★ ★ ★ ★

Acknowledgments

This Is Why We Lie wouldn't be complete without the help and support of so many wonderful people.

I want to start by giving huge thanks to my agent, Whitney Ross, and everyone at Irene Goodman Literary Agency who worked on this book in the early stages of its journey. Whitney, your optimism, commitment, and encouragement has been truly inspiring and I'm so grateful for everything you've done and everything you continue to do.

Many thanks to Connolly Bottum, who embraced this story and these characters so fully. Being part of the Inkyard family is a dream come true and I am eternally grateful for this. Connolly, thank you for seeing something special in these characters and for guiding me to bring out the very best in them.

To the entire Inkyard/HarperCollins team, thank you for all of the hard work and dedication you've put into bringing this book to life!

To my parents, Angela and Elio, whose support, love, and

openness is unparalleled. I'm so lucky to share adventures with you and it's an honor to make you proud.

To my husband, James, thank you for all the hours, days, weeks, months, years of everything. No one makes a spreadsheet better than you do…and you know it!

To my daughter, Sophia, thank you for being the whirlwind of joy, love, and laughter that you are. You are my inspiration and my most incredible blessing.

To my family and friends, thank you for being part of this journey and for all the support you've given me every step of the way. Lepores, Nelsons, Carters, Chimbwandas, Sue, Clive, Roger, Trisha, Nan, Shirley, Maureen, and Rachel, your words have been much appreciated. And in loving memory of my grandfather Brian, who bought me way more than 'leven books.

To everyone reading this, thank you. I'm so glad you chose this book, and I hope you enjoyed it!